# Magic Misfire

## The Raven Academy Book Two

A. Caprice

Cover Art by Dar Albert

# THE PROPHECY THAT STARTED THIS WHOLE MESS...

*She who is born to the witch who comes this year will be the alpha and the omega.*

*She will be the bringer of peace, and the advance guard of war.*

*Many magical creatures will die in the battle.*

*That which saves us will also destroy.*

*That which destroys, can also be destroyed.*

*She has the power to end our world.*

*Quidquid id est, timeo de ignotis.*

# Chapter One

As plans went, Dante's sucked the big one.

"You're never in charge of plans again," I screamed, dodging one of the tentacles of the monster trying to take my head off.

"Agreed." Gareth plucked *my* battle axe from the ground and chopped off one of the slimy arms.

Two more popped back in its place.

"Stop doing that!" Jesus, the thing had started with just the three arms, and now it was as handsy as a politician on a campaign trail.

Gareth growled, the sound especially deep and frightening coming from the demon. "I tear things apart. That's what I do."

"Perhaps," Professor Bane said, neatly sliding in front of me and putting a stunning spell on one of the tentacles, "you could try to use your head for once and not mindlessly chop at the regenerating monster?"

"I'm almost there, guys." Dante was hunched over a laptop in the corner, a red cord connecting his computer to the council's mainframe. It was strange to think in this world of magic I'd found myself thrown into that witches and warlocks still used such ordinary devices like computers, but there you had it.

All the information of the council's doings, their management of The Raven Academy, was trapped in the mainframe, just waiting for Dante's hacking to get it out.

I took a slimy punch to the jaw and staggered sideways.

At least, I hoped the information we needed was there. Or else this would be a very dangerous, and messy, waste of time.

"Almost there..." Dante muttered.

And we were almost dead. The monster the council had left to protect the premises wanted nothing more than to pull us all into a big hug and squeeze the life out of us. I could see it in its beady, purple eyes.

Well, I could see it in one of the eyes. Another eye showed definite hunger pangs. The rest just looked bored.

I got in my fighting stance. Centered myself, felt my intention gather in my core. We needed this intel and I wouldn't let octo-bastard stop us. If the prophecy was right, the world could be coming to an end. Soon.

And I might have something to do with it.

That was a possibility I couldn't fathom. So instead of wondering how I, unimportant, little Delaney Jones from Detroit, mediocre witch and cream puff connoisseur, could hold the balance of the world in my hands, I lowered my head and kept fighting.

I raised my hands, watching with joy as my energy lit them up like firecrackers after the Superbowl. I directed that energy into the monster's eye.

It blinked. Swiped a tentacle across what I guess was its face. Then swiveled a glare in my direction.

Shit. After a couple months at the academy, I could create some spells now, but there was no power behind them. I was next to useless in a magical fight, not unless I got angry and went Hulk with my magic.

But I had no control when that happened, and I could hurt one of the guys instead of the monster. There was also the problem that I couldn't make myself feel the level of rage required. It was something that just happened naturally, usually when one of my guys pissed me off by not telling me something I had a right to know.

And when it came to Dante, Gareth and Bane, I wanted to know everything.

So, with my magic next to useless, I went to my next best tool. I'd trained as a fighter in Detroit's underground cage fighting scene, and my fists and street smarts had gotten me out of more trouble than I wanted to think about.

I blocked another tentacle, ignoring the dull pain in my shoulder. I let the little suction cups at the end of the octo-bastard's arm stick to my palm, tightened my fingers around it. Then I ran like there was only one slice of pie left in the cafeteria, straight at the monster.

"Delaney!" Gareth bellowed. He lurched toward me and was blocked by three arms.

"Miss Jones," the professor hollered in his snooty, yet oh so sexy British accent, "stop this inst—"

I took aim. Went into my best baseball slide. Right between the monster's legs. It leaned forward, blinking at me through the large vee its legs made. I popped to my feet behind it. And gave the thing a wedgie with its own arm.

It made a sound somewhere between a dying bullfrog and a moose in heat. It yanked its tentacle from my hand, snapped its legs together, and gave me such a reproachful look I almost felt bad.

Almost.

The distraction was enough. Gareth and Bane launched synchronized magical attacks. I don't know if they'd discussed it, but both had decided to go with freezing the creature. Its legs turned into icicles first, and it toppled to the floor, making the room shake. It pulled its tentacles into its body, like it was trying to preserve body heat, but Gareth and Bane were relentless. I lobbed a couple of spells at the thing, too, knowing they had next to no effect, but I didn't want to appear useless in front of my men.

They tended to get scrunched up expressions of worry on their faces when they were reminded of how bad I was at being a witch.

Well, Dante looked worried. Gareth usually looked scarily determined, like he wanted to enlist me in a magic bootcamp until I got it right. And that wouldn't be fun for anyone, least of all me. And Bane...

Well, he looked annoyed, as though he thought I was being difficult on purpose. I was pretty sure it was a self-defense mechanism on his part. Being annoyed with me was much easier than admitting to his feelings. The deep, mushy ones that would make his world a sad and colorless place if anything happened to me.

But irritation could just be irritation and I *might* have been doing a bit of projection. Or wishful thinking.

Unfortunately for me, his condescending, exasperated demeanor was a real turn on. I wanted nothing more than to slide the tie from his neck, put a ruler in his hand, and demand he discipline his bad student.

More unfortunately for me, my naughty feelings weren't limited to Bane. Gareth and Dante also played leading roles in my midnight fantasies. And one night, Dante had actually been a participant in non-imaginary smexy times. Each man was panty-wetting hot and sweet in his own way. A deadly combination. And an impossible choice.

I was so fucked, and not in the good way.

The monster stopped moving. Bane murmured an incantation, and leather straps appeared, wrapping themselves around the fallen form, tying it up like a neat package.

I brushed my hands together, "Well, that was fun. Yea for teamwork!"

Bane straightened his tie. He sighed heavily as he shot me a disapproving look. "Really, Miss Jones, when will you stop resorting to human methods of battle? You've been at the academy for two months now. Your magic should be improving."

Gareth cleaned purple slime off the blade of the battle axe. "Her methods were effective." He prowled up to me, so close I could feel the heat from his bare chest.

Gareth liked to fight without a shirt. With his luminous dark skin stretching over acres of muscles and decorated with swirling black tribal tattoos, it was distracting as hell. But I wouldn't be asking him to cover up any time soon.

He cupped my chin, his thumb stroking my lower lip. "Good job, pet. Are you injured anywhere?"

My breath caught in my throat at the concern I saw in his eyes. As much as I liked to pretend it was only lust between the four of us, it wasn't. It was worse than that. Feelings were developing, and I wasn't a feelings kind of person. And with three men?

I was doubly fucked.

Why did they all have to pull at my heartstrings in their uniquely screwed up ways?

I shook my head, unable to speak. I shifted my weight, not liking how his gaze seemed to see past my walls. Yet some perverse part of me hoped he'd knock them all down to rubble.

"Got it!" Dante shouted. He looked up, a triumphant smile creasing his face. He looked at the fallen monster. "Oh. You got it." His gaze travelled, landed on me and Gareth, his smile falling faster than an underbaked souffle. "If you'd take your hands off my girl, maybe you could do something useful, like get us the hell out of here." He stood, showing me his back as he wrapped up his cables and slid his laptop into his bag. Showing me he wasn't just annoyed with the demon.

My heart pinched. He and I needed to talk. Just because we'd done the horizontal tango didn't mean I was ready to be his—I swallowed—girlfriend. I looked at Gareth and Bane. I wasn't ready to pick any of them, although to be fair, Bane didn't seem to want to be picked.

But I'd seen the way he'd look at me at times, like he wanted to eat me up with a spoon. Or his tongue. It must be the whole professor-student thing he didn't want to tread into. It couldn't be that he didn't actually like me.

I was delightful, after all.

"I'll do it," Bane said. He closed his eyes, held his hands up, and the air shimmered in front of him, thickening. The odd distortion widened, stretching long enough to form a small door.

"You have to teach me how to do that." The ability to create your own portal was high-level stuff I probably wasn't ready for. But if anyone needed an escape hatch, it was me. Ever since finding out I was a witch, attacks on my life had become more common than I liked.

Okay, any attack was one more than I wanted. But being a witch was my life now, and I needed to be able to roll with it.

Too many people thought I was some Chosen One from some stupid, vague-ass prophecy. The one who would either destroy the world or save it.

No pressure, right?

It seemed there were beings who wanted the world to end, and wanted to kill me to be sure I didn't save it. And even though Bane denied it, I had to assume there were good witches and warlocks who worried I would be the harbinger of death and also set their sights on ending the threat. Ending me.

The ethics of that were murky as hell, but if it wasn't me with a target on my back, I could see the temptation to eliminate the possible world-ending threat.

"You need to be able to perfectly visualize the place you want to travel to." Bane crossed his arms. "Where did you leave your divination textbook in your room? Are there any dirty clothes on your floor? Is your water glass two inches from the edge of the nightstand or three?"

"Uhh..." I didn't know what was more unnerving. That he knew roughly how my room looked or that I'd forgotten. Had I left last night's clothes on the floor? I couldn't remember.

"Exactly," he said. "Until you can visualize with exact detail the room you want to teleport to, be able to see it like a picture, you will not be attempting portals."

An image as precise as a photo did pop into my mind. It was the only place I could remember with the exactness he required. A broken picture frame. The ragged edge of a comforter from a make-shift bed peeking out of the closet.

My heart thudded, sluggishly pulsing my blood through my body.

It was a place I never wanted to go to again.

"Right." I cleared my throat, forcing a smile. "We'll just use yours, shall we?" I slipped past him and darted through his portal.

There was a moment of disorientation, a blinding light, and then I was standing in Bane's office at the academy. I scooted sideways to make way for my fellow portal travelers while peering around. I wondered if I had time to take a quick peek through Bane's desk while—

Gareth strode into the room. "I hate warlock portals," he grumbled. "My trips to the lower world are so much more fun."

I didn't have much time to ponder why portals between species would be different before Dante jumped into the room, falling into the desk, quickly followed by a wide-eyed Bane. A streak of purple slime splashed across his cheek and the back of his hair stuck out at an odd angle.

"The thing defrosted," Dante explained as he straightened. "We, uh, had to make a quick exit."

"Well, what did we learn? Was breaking into the council headquarters worth it?" I twisted the thick silver ring on my thumb. After I'd killed Thanness, a fellow student who'd been sent to kill me, I'd thought our chances of figuring out who'd hired him were next to nothing. Dante's plan had given me hope, but now I worried we'd find nothing except records of students' grades and disciplinary files. It wasn't like the council would include in their official records the details of an evil plot.

"Do you know how many terabytes I downloaded?" Dante shook his head. "Sorry, babe, but this isn't going to be a ready answer. It could take me weeks, months before I find anything."

*If* he found anything.

My heart sank.

Gareth crossed his arms. "I don't like waiting."

"Well, you can spend your time training Miss Jones." Bane circled behind his desk, pulling a handkerchief from his coat pocket. He sat in his chair and wiped his face clean of slime. "It is apparent she is still behind her peers."

Gareth's pupils changed shape, elongating before snapping back into place. I'd only seen it happen during times of high emotion... or when he thought about me. A sharp tingle snaked down my spine. He gave me a slow, dirty smile. "I look forward to it." And with a poof, he blinked out of existence.

"I hate when he does that," I grumbled.

Dante strolled in front of me. He bent and pressed his lips to the corner of my mouth, and I sighed. There was something about Dante that made me feel so safe. He was the kind of guy you could curl up in bed with and spend hours with cuddling, talking about your day, and he would happily listen.

And then take your mind off your day by doing rough, dirty things to you in that bed. I'd discovered that the sweet all-American guy had a decidedly dirty mind between the sheets, and I wasn't complaining. But none of my men were simple or easy to figure out.

"Don't worry, babe." He cupped the back of my head and kneaded my skull. I almost closed my eyes in bliss. "I won't be popping out of your life."

And he swaggered from the room, laptop bag tucked safely under his arm.

Leaving me alone with Bane.

I looked at him, hoping he, too, would leave me with some sweet words. Something to give me hope that the squishy feelings I had whenever I saw him weren't doomed to go unrequited.

His hooded gaze raked my skinny jeans, my tank top, before settling on my face. His piercing blue eyes stung me like an electric wire. "Miss Jones..."

I rocked onto the balls of my feet. "Yes?"

"I believe you have class in fifteen minutes. You'd best get moving." And he turned to his computer, powering it to life, a clear dismissal.

My shoulders rounded. I shouldn't be greedy. I had two beautiful, loyal men vying for my affection.

But damn, I wanted that third to complete the set.

# Chapter Two

Since the incident in the greenhouse when my entire class had almost drowned, Basics of Herbology had been relegated to the classroom. No hands-on learning at all. Professor Clovern had taken an extended leave of absence during his recovery, and the succession of substitute teachers had told us to read a chapter from our textbook each class.

If this had been high school, I would have dropped out all over again.

I yawned widely, belatedly remembering to cover my mouth.

"Another late night?" Hazel, my bestie and the smartest witch at Raven, although I might have been a tad bit biased, slunk over to my desk, keeping a watchful eye on the babysitter in the front. The sub looked up, looked back down at her novel. She didn't care what we did as long as we did it quietly.

"Early morning." We'd been prepping for the infiltration of the council since Dante had dragged my butt from bed at five. Bane had wanted to launch our stealth attack right when the council closed for the day and before their night security arrived. With the time change to Paris, that meant we had to give up our lunch hour.

I didn't want to think about what the a-game security was like if octo-bastard was the JV team.

Quincy joined us, sliding a brown paper bag across my desk like it was full of illegal drugs.

I peeked inside and couldn't contain my squeak of delight. A turkey sandwich lay inside with the cranberry sauce staining the wax paper wrapper. Next to it was a thick slice of... "Cook's butter pound cake," I breathed. My stomach rumbled in anticipation. "You guys are the best."

"We know," Hazel said.

Quincy nudged her shoulder with his own.

"I was getting to it," she whisper-hissed. She turned back to me. "Did you guys learn anything?"

I looked around as I unwrapped my sammie. Most other students were talking softly in small groups, not paying us any mind.

Or purposely ignoring me.

The first few days after the greenhouse flood had been rough. Backs had been turned on me. Whispered curses thrown my way. But while the other students weren't lining up to invite me out to party, the outright hostility seemed to have dwindled to just a few main, and obvious, culprits.

But getting shunned still annoyed me. Sure, I might have unwittingly read the spell that kick-started the flood, and yes, the dark magician who'd created it had been trying to kill me, but that still didn't make me responsible. But when a mob of people decided you were taboo, there was just no reasoning with them.

"Nothing yet," I murmured. "Dante has to go through the information we downloaded." Which might be why he was skipping this class yet again. But since the Academy now knew he was an undercover agent sent by a white lodge to investigate the disappearances of their graduates, I didn't think any teacher would be trying to give him detention.

A high-pitched giggle broke through the quiet. The substitute raised her head to look where Ophelia, one of the students who still reveled in making my life miserable, perched on her stool. The teacher sniffed then lowered her head back to her book.

"Just wanted to call and say thank you, daddy." Ophelia plucked a large bag from her desk and held it on her lap. "I love my present. How did you know I wanted the purse with the pink ostrich leather?"

I quirked my head. "Is she having a conversation with herself? That's weird, even for her."

Hazel rubbed her chin. "Uh, she's talking to her dad? That man, right there, in the hologram?" She frowned. "Of course she'd have the latest magical tech. Sometimes life just isn't fair."

I leaned closer to Hazel to see if her cheeks were flushed. Illness could explain her hallucination.

A shimmer of silver caught the corner of my eye. I leaned back. No silver. What the hell?

I stood and rounded the table to stand behind my friend. And there, hovering in front of Ophelia, was the image of an older man with the same evil-eyed squint that my nemesis wore. Okay, I might have made that last bit up, but there was definitely a family resemblance.

"Anything for my baby girl." He brought his hand up to look at his watch. It was strange. The image of the man was clear from only about the waist up, so when he lowered his arm again, it disappeared as though going out of frame.

"What is that?" I whispered. I darted back to my side of the desk to confirm that the image wasn't visible from the back.

Ophelia blew a kiss at what looked like nothing, then turned to me. "This is only the most sought after bag this year." She ran her hand along the feather laced shoulder strap. "It's a one-of-a-kind Gouverny. It's hand-stitched, has their signature platinum clasp, and uses only the finest, sustainable resources. Gouverny only made a hundred in this style, each one using different leathers or in different colors to make them all unique."

Hazel crossed one leg over the other and bobbed her foot. "Is that where you store all your butt plugs? I thought you'd need a bigger bag considering the size of the stick up your ass."

A snort of laughter escaped me even as I barely contained my eyeroll at the frou frou pink bag. My messenger bag carried more stuff *and* didn't mark me as a rich twat just waiting to be robbed. "What I meant was how was an image of your dad appearing in the middle of the air?"

"Oh." She gave up glaring at Hazel to turn to me. "That's just my Pic Portal." She shook her wrist, a heavy gold bracelet jingling. She tapped a wide oval medallion in the middle of the chain. "The charm here has been spelled to allow me to call up anyone who has another device. It's only the latest in witch technology. What?" She gave me a wide smile that didn't reach her eyes. "You don't have one?"

Okay, that was pretty damn cool, but I wasn't going to let it show I was impressed. I pulled my phone from my pocket. "Uh, yeah. It's called FaceTime. How disappointing that witch technology is just now joining the twenty-first century."

Quincy chuckled. Ophelia glared at him, and the tips of his ears went pink.

"It is *not* like FaceTime." Ophelia's face darkened. "I don't need a phone for starter's—"

"Just a bracelet," Hazel pointed out.

"And the holographic image can appear anywhere," Ophelia finished.

I held my phone to my left, to my right. "My image can appear anywhere, too." Now that I had it out, I huddled behind Hazel and Quincy and snapped a selfie. "Shoot," I said, examining the picture. "My hair's looking jacked today. Why didn't anyone tell me?"

"You students are supposed to be reading your textbook." The substitute sighed heavily, her gaze still down on her book. "You can talk after class."

Fair enough. I slid back onto my stool and pulled my lunch in front of me. If I couldn't mess with Ophelia, eating was a terrific second-best option.

I bit into the sourdough sandwich, letting the tang of the bread and the cranberries ease my lingering irritation. I might have moaned. All I know is I got a dirty look from the sub.

Then her eyes went wide and she patted her hair as she threw a vivacious smile over my shoulder.

I turned on my stool.

And choked on my bite of turkey.

The stranger slid across the room to me, his pale skin seeming to absorb the light. He pounded me on the back, a bit harder than necessary, and gave me a warm smile as the bit of food slid down my throat.

"Perhaps Herbology class isn't the best place to eat, yes?" he said. "You never know what poisonous herb might have left its remnants on your desks."

I nodded, mute. There was something about him that made me want to be as silent as a mouse and hope he moved on to other prey.

He glided up the aisle to the front of the room, his very presence stopping conversations whenever he passed.

He was handsome in a Lord of the Rings blond elf kind of way. He smiled with real warmth at those he made eye contact with.

But you could just tell something about this man was deadly.

"Vampire," Hazel whispered.

A shiver zigzagged down my spine.

An undead being. Frankly, I'd had enough of those.

He murmured a couple words to the substitute.

She blushed, tittering behind her hand. Then she gathered her things and exited the room.

"Good afternoon, class." The vampire took the substitute's seat. "I am Professor Khad Killough. I'll be taking over Professor Clovern's duties for the remainder of the year. I hope by that time we'll all have become good friends."

Ophelia smiled back at him, arching her back to jut out her breasts. "You can count on it."

Hmph. I wasn't so sure. The person who'd tried to kill me here at Raven was dead, but I had a feeling more would follow. Whoever had hired Thanness could pay someone else to target me. And until all of this was resolved, I wasn't trusting any new faces.

Even pretty ones like Killough's.

Especially the pretty ones.

The vamp's eyes flitted to her breasts, back to Ophelia's face, his smile deepening. It didn't look like he was buying what she was trying to sell.

Which made me like him a bit more. And also wonder if I should try that move with Bane. My boobs were decent. Maybe if I pressed them in his face his icy reserve would be stripped away. But I'd never been the coy, flirtatious type. And I didn't know if I could stomach the same amused rejection Killough had just delivered to Ophelia.

Hazel snorted. "This oughta be good," she whispered, then followed Quincy back to their desk.

Ophelia turned to glare back at me, like I'd been the snorter.

I lifted my hands in a 'wasn't me' gesture, but her eyes only got squintier. I don't think she'd forgiven me for the time I hugged her. It wasn't one of my fondest memories, either.

"Now, I know you've had some upheaval and are a bit behind in the lesson plan, but I'm certain if we focus and apply ourselves we can accomplish much this year."

A large sunflower sitting on the windowsill unfurled its petals, giving itself a little shimmy as it announced the hour. Killough glanced at it. "But I see today's class is already over. So read up on the uses of the sap of the Dragon's-blood tree, and I'll see you all Thursday."

The students burst into noisy chatter as they hit the hallway. "He's the first vampire professor at the Raven Academy," someone said in a hushed voice.

"It's a disgrace," another hissed.

"The Raven Academy has adopted a policy of non-discrimination against any magical beings," Ophelia said stiffly. "An open society. It's what my great-great-great-great-grandmother always envisioned when she founded the academy."

Rosamunde, one of Ophelia's lackeys, timidly raised her hand. "But is it safe? And with all those students disappearing, why add something else for us to worry about right now?"

"Students disappearing?" I stepped into the circle that naturally seemed to gather around Ophelia wherever she went. "What students are disappearing?" I hadn't noticed anyone missing from classes, but this was a big school. The group of students I recognized were only a small portion of it.

"Students who have graduated from the academy." Ophelia smirked. "It's not something you'll have to worry about. The chances of you graduating are zero."

I breathed a sigh of relief. Oh. Those students. I mean, it was awful, but I already knew about them. It would be worse if an entirely new group of people were disappearing. "Was that in the papers?" Dante might not be happy that his investigation was now open gossip. But maybe it could help him. He might learn more if people talked freely about it.

"It's been in all the papers." Ophelia turned on her heel and stalked down the hall. "Don't you read?" she shouted over her shoulder.

I let her go even though I wanted to grab her by the back of her designer blouse and take her to the ground. Maybe I could think of a good hex for her. Nothing too nasty. But a case of skin rash could be fun.

And it would be a way for me to practice magic. Bane would have to approve.

An image of him, frowning and folding his arms over his chest popped to mind.

Or not.

"When did news of the missing students get out?" I asked Hazel and Quincy.

"Last week. I think it was the day after we..." She swallowed and dropped her gaze to the floor.

Quincy threw his arm around her shoulders.

They'd both fully recovered physically from Thanness's magical attack, but I knew how powerless Hazel felt from being incapacitated. How scared.

I would have felt the same way.

"So the day after the council spoke with Dante and the others about his investigation," I said brightly, hoping to take her mind off of her near death. "I bet one of the councilmembers released the info to the papers. Maybe to spite the white lodge for planting Dante in the academy without telling them." I'd only met two council members before, but that seemed the type of petty, interfering thing they'd do. They wouldn't like that Dante was working here undercover as one of the academy's students.

"Well, I think it's a good thing." Hazel tromped down the hall toward their next class. "Put the graduate students on notice to watch their backs. I didn't like the thought of them being out there unaware of the threat like sitting ducks."

"Agreed." Quincy nodded stoutly.

I had to admit, I agreed with them, too. Dante and his lodge should have made it known former students were disappearing. Maybe some of them could have been saved. But now that the secret was out, would the white lodge pull Dante from the Raven Academy? His cover was blown with the Council, and, frankly, he hadn't learned much from his investigation pretending to be a student.

My stomach churned and the rest of the food in my sack didn't seem so appealing anymore. I couldn't imagine the academy without him. "Hey, can you guys take notes for me at divination? I've got to go talk to someone."

And without waiting for a response (it would be yes), I hurried down the hall and to the stairs leading to the dormitory.

The feeling that he would be gone, that he'd have disappeared on me without even saying goodbye, crawled up my throat and choked me.

Dante wouldn't do that. I knew it as well as I knew how to throw a right cross.

The feeling didn't make sense.

It wasn't rational.

But I broke into a trot, dread spiraling through me. Something felt wrong.

I was almost at a sprint by the time I reached his room. Without pausing to knock, not wanting to hear silence as my only response, I tested the knob and pushed the door open.

And found Dante hanging from the ceiling.

# Chapter Three

He wasn't hanging. Not technically. A fact I realized when Dante's eyes flew open at my shriek and he plummeted to the ground. Head first.

Yeah, he'd been floating upside-down. One leg crossed over the other in a pose eerily reminiscent of The Hanged Man in Tarot.

I rushed to his crumpled body. "Dante! Are you okay?"

He shook his head and pushed up onto his hands. "What the—"

"—hell kind of spell could do that to you?" I finished for him. I checked his body for other signs of mischief. Blisters. Bleeding. Warts. I didn't know what all a witch or warlock could do to his body, or why they'd want to. But I liked his body, and wanted to keep it spell-free.

"Do you feel okay? Do you think someone's taken control of your mind?" I reached for his shirt and yanked it up, checking the skin on his back. All clear.

"Not that I mind you taking my clothes off, but why are you peeling off my shirt?" His hair was rumpled, his eyes looked thick with sleep, but his smile was all Dante.

"To check for warts." I yanked upward on the t-shirt, and he obligingly raised his arms to help me pull it all the way off.

"Uh huh." He snaked a finger into my waistband and pulled me close. "And why would I have warts?"

I tumbled against his chest. His skin was warm as a furnace and he smelled of sunshine and clean clothes. But I wouldn't let that distract me. Not when magic was afoot.

"You were hanging upside down from the ceiling. Obviously someone put a spell on you. Unless..." I frowned. "Can you levitate?" Was this another bit of magic I was unaware of? Unaware of and probably too advanced for me to learn.

His face went carefully blank. "No. No, I don't levitate."

"Then you were spelled." I ran my hands over his shoulders. I'd like to say I was still checking for after-effects of magic, but a shirtless Dante was proving too great of a distraction. "Who do you think is after you? And why such a bizarre spell?"

He rolled to his feet, hauling me up with him. "I'm sure it was nothing. Just a prank. Don't worry about it."

"But—"

"I said don't worry about it." He softened his hard tone with a warm smile. "I like finding you in my room." He stepped close, his bare toes nudging my shoes. "I like it very much."

"Dante, this is serio—"

He covered my mouth with his own. His lips were warm. He tasted sweet. Comforting. Like how I imagined home should be. I clung to him, this big, solid man suddenly feeling much too vulnerable.

"Dante," I whispered. "Everyone is talking about your missing students."

He nibbled around my jaw and down my throat. "So?"

"And the academy knows you're here undercover." He sucked at the point where my pulse fluttered beneath my skin, and I tipped my head further back. "But you're not really undercover anymore."

"And?" He went lower, placing his mouth on my breast, sucking my nipple through my shirt and bra.

"Oh God." What had I been saying? Surely nothing more important than what Dante was doing. Wait. I wanted him to be able to keep doing it. Which meant—"But won't your white lodge pull you out of here? What would be the point if your cover is blown?"

I prayed there were multiple good reasons to keep him at the Raven Academy. That would keep him here as long as I was. I needed Dante.

Gareth would fight by my side. I had no worries when I was next to him. But he was still a mystery. A demon, and I knew next to nothing about him or his kind. I cared for him, but I couldn't count on him for any sort of emotional stability.

Professor Bane was also a great guy to have at my back. He was smart, determined, and I wanted him something bad. But he was as likely to push me away as hold me. I felt too topsy-turvy around him. Fielding his heated looks one moment and his dismissal another.

But Dante was my rock. My anchor. He was a lifeline in this new world I'd found myself in. If he left, I just might drown.

"My lodge has terminated my assignment." He raised his head, his dark eyes boring into mine. "They want me to return to headquarters and manage the investigation from there."

My heart plummeted faster than a skydiver. I tried to swallow, but my throat felt too swollen. He was leaving.

"Which is why I've taken a leave of absence." He cupped my cheek. "Don't you know yet? I'd never leave you. Not when you need me. And baby, you need me."

I whooshed out a breath, not liking how close that was becoming to the truth. I was Delaney Giantslayer Jones. I shouldn't need anyone.

Dante lowered his head, slanting his mouth across mine. All of my nerve endings fired to life with his kiss. His tongue in my mouth, his hands exploring my body, it was like air to me. Necessary. Essential to remain breathing and alive.

My chest ached with the hodge podge of emotions swirling through it. I didn't do gooey. I didn't do love. So obviously this couldn't be that silly emotion. Caring about someone was one thing, but allowing myself to become a slave to the intense devotion that fools in love seemed to succumb to just wasn't gonna happen. I couldn't do it.

But I could do Dante. I slid my hand under the waistband of his jeans and gripped his ass. I could make this simple, about pure pleasure, and straighten my head out later.

He groaned into my mouth, pressing his hardening erection against my belly.

Oh yes. I rubbed against him, feeling my panties get damp. We could do this very well, indeed.

But what the hell was that beeping sound?

Dante rested his forehead against mine, breathing heavily. “I have to take this call. Even though I’m on leave, I still work for the lodge.”

I tried to concentrate on his words. It was hard when all I wanted to do was rip his pants off and ride him into the sunset. But the fog eventually cleared.

His watch was beeping. Signifying a call. From his bosses.

I removed my hands from all inappropriate places. “Be sure to ask them about protections you can put up against spells against you.”

He guided me to his door. “It was just someone’s stupid idea of a joke,” he reassured me. “Don’t give it another thought.”

I shot him the smile he wanted. Nodded. But as I closed his door behind me, I straightened my shoulders.

Bad enough I had a target on my back.

I wasn't going to let some asshole put one on Dante's. Not on my watch.

It was time to get down to business.

# Chapter Four

Before the Raven Academy, I think I'd been in a library only twice in my life. The first time I'd been seeking refuge when Billy Maloney and his gang of eight-year-old bullies threatened to rip the feathers from my hair. Even at that young age I'd been rocking my hair fashion choices.

I'd raced into the Detroit Public Library, lost myself in a maze of stacks, and climbed to the top of one until the boys had grown bored with their search and wandered away.

The second time I'd been seven years older, and needed someplace private to make-out with Eddy Piolo. Which had been a mistake as most fifteen-year-old snosh sessions were.

His kisses had been wet and sloppy and he'd groped my breasts like he was torqueing a socket wrench. Instead of suffering through that unpleasantness, I really should have looked around at the time and realized the amazing wealth of knowledge that had surrounded me.

Libraries rocked. Especially magical ones where I only had to whisper a search request into the card catalog, and the little notecards with book names and locations came floating out.

I twirled a lock of hair from my ponytail around my finger, the new color bold against my skin. I'd dyed it Supergirl blue this morning, and it only served to reinforce my determination to save Dante. Supergirl wouldn't sit back while her bae was in trouble. Even if he swore he didn't need saving.

Hazel flopped into the wide armchair across from me. "You'll never guess what you missed in C and D."

C and D was the abbreviation most students used for Magical Combat and Defense. I just called it hell. With my lack of control, I was too scared to go hard with most of the spells. I might burn a hole right through someone with what was supposed to be a simple stinging spell.

Quincy settled in one of the other two chairs that made up our corner of the library.

Yes, it was our corner. We'd claimed it until we graduated. Or were kicked out, in my case. Any of the other students who complained could just deal with it.

"Did you learn how to block being magicked by someone from a distance?" I asked. "Because that's what I need right now."

Hazel frowned, her dark eyebrows drawing together under her widow's peak. "Why? Has something else happened?"

"You could say that." I told them about how I'd found Dante. I reached into my messenger bag and pulled out a card. "He thinks whoever spelled him was just pulling a prank, but he looked just like the picture in this Tarot Card. The Hanged Man. It was creepy." I shook off the memory of my fear. "The card means surrender. The ultimate sacrifice. I'm not going to let Dante become a sacrifice."

Quincy took the card from my hand and examined it. He nodded to Hazel.

"He's right," she said. "It can also represent a traitor." She dug her teeth into her bottom lip. "You don't think..."

"No." There was a hell of a lot I didn't know here, but I did know Dante was no traitor. He was loyal to a fault. I trusted him completely.

"Maybe it was supposed to be a warning to him?" She shrugged, her black page boy brushing her shoulders. "That he needs to keep a look out for someone trying to stab him in the back? Metaphorically, of course," she hurried to add.

My stomach clenched. Even if Hazel was right, that still meant there was a threat against him.

Quincy shifted. "Maybe it was just a joke. It didn't hurt him after all."

Hazel and I fell silent. When Quincy did speak, we tended to listen. I wanted to believe him, but the consequences could be too devastating if he was wrong.

"Let's hope you and Dante are right, but in the meantime, I want to find a way to protect him." I pulled one of the books I'd found toward me. "This one says he should carry around snakeroot, but I have no idea where to find that. I would have asked Professor Clovern, but..."

"With him gone from Herbology class, you don't want to ask the new vampire hottie." Hazel nodded in sympathy. "He does look intimidating."

I ignored that. Professor Killough didn't intimidate me. He just... unsettled me. There was a difference.

"This book says black obsidian can protect against sorcery." I narrowed my eyes, trying to remember. "I wonder if that voodoo shop in the French Quarter carries that stone."

"Another night at the bars?" Hazel whooped.

Quincy grumbled like an old dog roused from his nap. He hadn't enjoyed our night of boozing and carousing as much as me and Hazel.

Or he hadn't enjoyed seeing her dance with other men. The jury was still out on that one for me.

"We'll see." I wasn't eager to have Dante get all pissy again for me sneaking out of the academy. Though the results of our fight had been delightful.

I flipped open another book and rubbed my forehead. There had to be an answer in one of these damn things.

"Are you okay?" Hazel asked.

"Yeah, just getting a headache from all this reading."

"Does that happen a lot?" she asked. "I've noticed that you, uh, aren't fond of doing our reading assignments for classes."

I slouched in my chair. "Is it that obvious?"

"Only to those who know you well," she said diplomatically.

I slapped the book shut. "When I was in sixth grade, one of my teachers thought I had dyslexia. She went to my dad, saying I should get tested, that there were ways to help me, but..."

The back of my eyes burned. Which was stupid. It had happened a long time ago and I'd already known my dad was a selfish prick. Special classes might have meant money wasted that would have been better spent on beer.

"Anyway." I shrugged. "I forced myself to keep going through the homework until the letters sorted themselves out but I still don't enjoy reading. If they'd just get some of these textbooks into audio, I'd be set." I smiled, like it was no big deal. Because, in the grand scheme of things, it wasn't.

"Maybe you just haven't read the right books." Hazel chewed on her bottom lip, her eyes going distant.

"Doubtful." I held up the book in my lap and read the spine. "But the right book sure isn't going to be *Warding Off Esoteric Attacks.*"

"There you are!"

I started, dropping the heavy book on my thigh, and winced.

Ophelia stomped up to us, face red, and looking angry enough to spit nails. I'd never really understood that expression until now.

"Do you know what you've done?" she ground out. She stopped before me, hands on her hips, eyes narrowed.

"Judging by your reaction, something awesome." I gave her a wide smile. "I do like to irritate you, Ophelia."

It didn't have to be that way, but she'd come at me first. A bitch for a bitch, I liked to say.

"This is what we wanted to talk to you about," Hazel said. She grimaced at me with sympathy.

"What's happened?" I asked.

"Only the worst thing ever!" Ophelia leaned down and stabbed her finger at my chest. "Because you weren't in class today, Professor Klingor made you my partner in our final."

"We have finals already?" That news was almost worse than being partnered with the Wicked Witch. Almost.

"It's a practical test," Hazel explained. "It could be fun. You have to successfully attack your partner before the end of term. He wanted to take the combatives out of the classroom. Said it wasn't a realistic learning environment in there since everyone was prepared to defend against attacks in class. So," she said, the corners of her eyes crinkling devilishly, "you have three weeks to spell Ophelia. I can't wait to see it."

Quincy nudged her.

"Yes, yes, there are ground rules." She bent and pulled a piece of paper from her bag and handed it to me. "A list of the dos and don'ts in order to get a passing grade."

I scanned the paper. No attacking when your partner's back was turned. No spells that incurred permanent damage. No spells that put your partner in danger. Blah, blah, blah.

Ophelia tore the paper from my hand. "I don't want you as my partner. I don't want my grade to depend on you. I'm the descendant of Morgana Ravencroft, founder of this academy. And you"—she sneered—"you just don't belong here."

Hazel popped to her feet. Her widow's peak dipped dangerously down to her eyebrows. "Are you forgetting why the two of you were partnered? Oh yeah, 'cause you tattled on her like a little bitch. 'Professor Klingor, Delaney didn't come to class today,'" she mimicked in a high falsetto.

Ophelia took a step in Hazel's direction, and I raised my leg as a barrier. "This is a library," I said with all the condescension I could muster. "Would great grandmama Morgana approve of you starting a fight here?"

She clenched her hands. "I'm not the one who started this fight, but I damn well will be the one to finish it." And with a swirl of shiny, caramel-colored hair, she stomped off.

Hmpf. As last words went, she got in some damn good ones.

I looked at her retreating back and sighed.

Ophelia and I in school-sanctioned combat, trying to out spell the other.

Oh, joy. Nothing could go wrong with that.

Quincy stiffened. Hazel and I shot each other uneasy looks.

"Something wrong?" I asked.

He flipped his phone around so we could see the screen. A headline from the Magical Times was in large print at the top.

*Explosion in Dublin Has Authorities Scrambling to Erase Traces of Magic*

Hazel grabbed the phone and scanned the article. "It says two warlocks dragged a badger shifter into a pub and tried to use him as a dartboard. Other shifters found out and stormed the bar, and, well..." Her eyes flicked back and forth over the small screen.

"And?" I asked.

"And they blew it up." She handed the phone back to Quincy. "Witnesses said there were spells flying back and forth. No one knows which one did the deed." She swallowed. "Four witches and one shifter were killed."

My stomach clenched. "It's starting, isn't it? These are the first few battles before we get a full-on war."

Hazel fiddled with the seam of her jeans. "I don't like that it's witches starting it. If it was an enemy coming for us, it would be easier. But when it's our own side who are the bad guys..."

"They are not our side." I scooted to the edge of my chair. "They might be witches, too, but that doesn't mean we're all on one team. Whoever the bad guys are, we'll fight them. And we'll win." I looked each of them in the eyes, trying to give them a confidence I didn't feel.

Hazel was right, though. It sucked that witches were the ones who attacked an innocent shifter. It tainted them all. Unless the shifter wasn't innocent. You couldn't trust the media to tell it like it was. Maybe the badger had done something to cause the attack? Either way, the coming battle would be hard enough, but with bad actors on both sides, it made it damn near impossible to know who the enemy was. An army of witches was being formed, but that didn't mean other magical creatures were innocent. I'd already had my own run in with a shifter, and he definitely wasn't on the side of right. There seemed to be a high number of people who wanted this war, for reasons I could barely fathom.

Money and power were the obvious suspects, but it felt like there was a deeper reason.

And if only I could figure out what it was, I might be able to end this before any more lives were lost.

# Chapter Five

The days were growing shorter, and full dusk had fallen by the time I made my way to Gareth's gym after dinner. The humid air was soft against my skin, and I took my time, enjoying the stroll through the academy's grounds.

So much had happened in the past couple months. Things I never would have believed possible just a year ago. It was nice to be able to slow my pace for once, catch my breath, even if Gareth would be grumpy because I was a couple minutes late.

But a grumpy Gareth was a sexy Gareth.

I plucked a magnolia blossom from the ground under one of the trees. The scent was heady, and I inhaled deeply. It must have been magic that kept these trees blooming all the time. No regular gardener was that good.

Something rustled behind me.

I spun, but nothing was there. Just the trees, the lights from the pool in the distance, and the outline of the school squatting behind it.

Pursing my lips, I turned back on my path, my stride a bit quicker. It was probably just a bird. Or a squirrel. Something harmless and cute. But with stories of attacks and pubs exploding, it didn't hurt to pick up my pace. I was close to Gareth's gym. If necessary, it was only one short sprint around a hedge and I'd be able to see it.

The rustling sounded again. Closer.

I spun, getting in my fighting stance. The flower looked absurd in my hand so I tossed it down. "Is anyone there? Show yourself."

I heard Bane's voice in my head, critiquing my defenses. I gritted my teeth, because he wasn't being overly complimentary, even in my imagination, but I gathered my intention for a shielding spell into my core.

Nothing appeared. My shoulders dropped. I was going to feel like a fool if I threw up a shield for a harmless, little rabbit. Which was really all it could be. The academy had its own protective shields. Nothing threatening from the outside world was supposed to get in.

Not unless it walked through the front door. Like a student or professor.

I rubbed my arms. I hated not trusting anyone but my close circle. Hated that through an accident of birth people thought I was a Chosen One. I set my shoulders. But it was what it was. No use bitchin' about it now.

The rustling sounded above my head, and I jerked my glance up. From what looked like a long distance away, a speck of light appeared. It drifted lazily down and down until it hovered about an arm's span away.

I chuckled. A firefly. I'd been afraid of insects. Another light blinked into existence. Another. They danced around me, creating mesmerizing patterns, until if felt like I was inside a glowing whirlwind. "So pretty," I whispered. I reached out my hand. I didn't want to catch one, but needed to be closer to the beauty.

My eyes widened as one of the bugs darted close and landed on my finger.

"Mother chucker!" I shook my hand then cradled it to my belly. Fuck me, that stung. Like the little guy had been attached to a car battery.

Another one drifted close. Its round body flashed red before returning to its warm glow.

I ducked beneath it and pulled up short before I ran into a wall of them. Pain arced from the back of my shoulder down to my toes, and I fell to the ground, my knees giving out beneath me.

These weren't fireflies. Damn it, why had I expected anything to be normal here. Another shock tore through me. I twisted, and threw up a wall of shimmering light between me and the little bastard. It bounced off and buzzed in an angry circle.

"Hah!" Triumph swirled in my veins. I'd actually called up the appropriate spell at the right time. My training was paying off.

Pain lashed my back. I stumbled forward. My shield wavered but held. I turned and pressed the magic wall against that side of the bugs. And that's when I realized the flaw in my spell. I'd created a wall when I needed a cone to surround my body. The zapping buggers had too many angles of attack left to them.

I spun this way and that, desperate to keep my shield between me and the bugs. It didn't work.

A shock numbed my left calf muscle. I went down on one knee. Exhaustion tugged at me. Each time I was hit, it took a little more out of me. I spread my hands, and my shield obligingly split into two long walls. I was shielded on both sides of my body.

I would have been uber impressed with myself, except it still wasn't enough. I was still open on the front and back and from above. I couldn't stay here. I staggered to my feet. I had to make a run for it.

I sucked down a deep breath and pressed my shoulders together. Took aim in the direction where the bugs seemed least dense. And bolted forward, pushing my shield in front of me.

The bugs were smart. They'd learned to avoid my magic. They separated before me... and swarmed on my back.

I screamed. The pain was excruciating. I tried to push through it, to keep putting one foot in front of the other. They were hitting me so fast, I didn't feel the individual shocks. My body was one giant live wire. My vision blurred. My lungs squeezed. But I kept moving my feet.

Until I finally realized I wasn't going anywhere. I was face down in the dirt, my legs shifting uselessly. With the last of my energy, I rolled to my back, gathered my intent, and threw out a shield above me.

It wavered, looking much to thin, but it did the job. With the earth at my back, the bastards had more limited access, buzzing down to the ground and around my wall to get at my sides.

I whimpered. What I needed was a spell for the earth to swallow me whole, take me away from the pain. At this moment, being dead and buried seemed a preferable alternative. My body jerked at the next shock. The next. My shield blipped, like it was shorting out. Came back online. Then disappeared for good.

My hands fell to the ground, my eyes sinking shut. I was out of juice. I had nothing left to give. I waited for the swarm to take me.

And waited.

I pushed one eyelid up. Making even that tiny muscle move took a Herculean effort. But nothing glowed above me. The bugs were gone.

"Delaney." Gareth dropped to one knee by my side. His tattoos moved at a breakneck speed and a deep divot marred his forehead.

Gareth looked worried, and he never looked worried. He gathered me in his arms, held me tight to his chest, and ran for his cottage.

"What… what…?" What the hell were those things, my brain wanted to know. But my lips wouldn't form the words.

"Hush." He kicked open his front door and shouldered us through as the door bounced back. He laid me down on something firm and cool then disappeared.

A mat. I rested my palm on it. We were in his gym. A nice enough place to nap, I supposed.

"Delaney." He tapped my cheek. More of a slap, really, one I didn't appreciate.

"Go 'way. Sleep."

He hit me harder.

Mother fu—

"Drink," he said. He cradled the back of my neck and lifted my head from the floor. He held a glass bottle to my lips and tipped it up.

I had no choice. It was either drink or drown. The liquid was thick, almost like a smoothie, but nowhere near as sweet.

I turned my head away. "Gah. Gross."

"I don't care if you like it." His grip firmed on my nape and he held me immobile, pressing the bottle back to my mouth. "Drink."

I held my breath, hoping that if I couldn't smell it, I wouldn't be able to taste it, either.

I tasted it. Every bitter, acrid swallow. It was like drinking motor oil tinged with eucalyptus. I couldn't take it anymore. I jerked up to sitting and pushed the bottle away. "Enough."

Gareth closed his eyes, blowing out a long breath. "Your energy is back. I got to you in time."

Huh. I did feel better. I swiped the bottle from Gareth's lax hand and took another tiny sip, ignoring my gag reflex. If it worked, it worked. "What were those things?"

"Minges." He opened his eyes, his irises looking like liquid gold. "They suck the chi from a person, their magical lifeblood." He ground his jaw. "They shouldn't have been able to get inside academy grounds."

"Yeah, I seem to hear that a lot." I took another sip. "Do you think this was an attack? Someone trying to hurt me?"

He scraped a hand across his jaw. "Perhaps. It could have been an accident. Magical wards aren't one hundred percent effective. I'll look into it."

I raised the bottle to my mouth, but Gareth took it from my hand. "A bit of this will save you from the effects of a minge attack. Too much is dangerous."

"What is it? A potion?" And why did he have it already brewed? Were minge attacks that common?

"No. It's demon whiskey." He plugged the neck of the bottle with a cork. "But someone discovered it helps with the effects of minges, xuihei, and scarbers attacks. How do you feel?"

I rolled my shoulders, wiggled my toes. "Surprisingly good." It was like the attack had never happened. I pushed to my feet. Did I want to ask what the xui- and scar-things were? I pursed my lips. No, I did not.

Gareth strode across the gym, pausing next to the wall covered in swords. He placed his palm on the wood beneath a katana, and a panel slid open revealing rows of bottles. He returned the rotgut he'd poured down my throat to one of the shelves and then closed the makeshift bar.

"You keep booze in your gym?" And why had I never known this? A little after-training drink wouldn't have gone amiss all these nights I'd been here. Me and Gareth, sweaty from our workout, sharing a glass together, seeing where it led. I chewed on my bottom lip. Perhaps rubbing each other down, letting him massage my sore muscles as I—

"Of course." He cocked his head. "Where do you keep it?"

My cheeks went hot. So not the right time for naughty daydreams. "Uh, I don't. I wait for guys to give me drinks."

His pupils flashed, darkening his eyes, and I could feel his growl deep in my belly. Mentioning other guys to Gareth probably wasn't the smartest of ideas.

"I see." He stalked toward me. Energy seemed to crackle from his skin. "Well, now that you're feeling better, I have a job to do. Let's get to work."

# Chapter Six

I got to my feet and rolled my aching shoulder. I'd almost been able to fully deflect Gareth's magical attack that time. I was getting quicker in throwing up my wards.

As if reading my optimism, Gareth said, "Close doesn't count."

"Except in horseshoe and hand grenades," I muttered. "Yeah, yeah, but I'm getting there."

He folded his arms over his chest, clad in a tight black T-shirt that looked like it was losing the fight against his muscles. "You are improving. But you need to improve more."

The demon wasn't much of a motivational speaker, but he was a monster in the ring, and I was learning so much from him I couldn't complain.

I bobbed back and forth on my feet, trying to jack up my energy levels. My chicken Kiev from dinner sat heavily in my stomach, and the demon ale mixing with it didn't help.

If I never learned another drop of magic, at least I could say I'd had some damn fine meals at the Raven Academy.

"Gareth," I began as he circled around me. "Do you know any protections against someone trying to spell you from afar? Something beyond carrying protective charms in your pocket?"

He tilted his head. A tattoo of three interconnecting lines waved on the side of his neck. I never got used to his tats moving on his skin, but it was beautiful to watch. "Do you worry your opponent in your magical combat test will launch an illegal attack?"

My bobbing paused. "You know about that?"

"I know about much."

That I could believe. And yet I still knew so little about him.

"Well, this time it's not about me." I exhaled slowly, drawing my protective intentions into my center.

Gareth wasn't above a surprise attack, either. "I'm worried about Dante. I think someone is trying to hurt him."

He grunted. Shrugged.

"You've fought beside this man," I reminded him. "We're all supposed to be a team."

I didn't see the streak of red until it filled my vision and I was flying backwards. I hit the padded floor, my breath knocked from me.

In a blink, Gareth was there. Lowering over me. Pressing every inch of his hard body to mine. "I could make you forget him." His voice was husky, and I lost my breath for a whole other reason.

"You feel the connection between us." He dragged the rough pad of his finger down my throat, across my collar bone, the tip of it settling at the top of the valley between my breasts. "I know you do. Forget the pup. Let me show you what a demon can do. You'll never want another human again."

My blood burned like fire in my veins. I put my hands on his hips, but to push him away or pull him tight, I didn't know.

"This isn't helping with my training," I said, my voice reedy.

"I decided you need a more hands-on approach to learning." He pumped his finger between my cleavage, the movement putting me in mind of so much more. Of him pumping into me somewhere else. Or of me holding my breasts for him as he slid his cock through them. I knew that was a thing, I'd just never understood the allure of it until now.

My nipples pebbled.

This felt right. And so familiar. Just like in my dreams. My thighs widened on their own, letting his hips sink between them.

A growl rumbled through his chest, raising the hair on my body, and I opened my mouth to moan just as he took my lips.

His kiss was nothing like Dante's. The only thing they had in common was how good both kisses felt. But whereas Dante teased and coaxed my tongue to take up the dance, Gareth asked for nothing.

He took. Demanded my surrender. He rested his palm on the base of my throat as he plundered my mouth, the gesture possessive, controlling, and somehow reassuring. Under Gareth, I felt vulnerable yet protected. Like prey, yet cherished at the same time. It was hot and confusing as hell.

He nipped at my lip, and my adrenalin surged. I planted one foot on the ground, pushed off, and rolled, taking him beneath me.

He chuckled darkly when I pressed his wrists into the mat. "Nice move, pet."

"I have lots of good moves." I straddled his hips. His erection nestled right where I needed it, feeling so good I didn't want to move.

His eyes went black. "I can't wait to learn them all." A tattoo on the corner of his throat shimmied.

I traced the black whorls with my finger. "Is this magic or a demon thing?"

"Both. Demons have our own kind of magic." He planted one thick hand on my ass. "My tats tell the story of my life, and that keeps changing."

I pulled his shirt up to reveal his stomach and chest. Saw more swirling lines of black ink. I bent and traced one with my tongue. It tingled, like tonguing the end of a 9-volt battery. "Are the symbols a demon language?"

His fingers dug into my flesh. He wanted me to explore, I could tell, but oh, it was a struggle letting me take the driver's seat. "Yes. One very few beings know anymore."

If I was going to learn a second language, that seemed like a good choice. I'd love to be able to read Gareth's story, learn everything there was to know about him. "No demon girlfriends back in lower world?" I asked him. How anyone hadn't jumped on this man yet, I couldn't understand.

How I'd waited so long to jump on him was pretty awe-inspiring. I must have had the self-restraint of a nun. But no longer. I flicked my tongue over one flat nipple then scored it with my teeth. A tiny niggle of guilt wormed into my heart. It was so damn confusing wanting more than one man. And it wasn't that long ago I'd had my lips pressed to Dante's. But all my guys knew where I stood. That I liked all of them. That I couldn't seem to choose.

Gareth grabbed my ponytail and yanked my head back. "I wouldn't be here if I did." He tossed me to my back like I weighed nothing and flipped on top of me.

"Why are you here?" I ran my hands over his shoulders. Up his neck. Over his shaved head. It was like once I'd started touching him, I couldn't stop.

He pressed his cock against my pussy. "I've been wanting to be *here* since the moment I saw you."

I smothered a giggle. I wasn't a giggler, and I wouldn't let myself become one just because a sexy demon made silly puns. "I mean, why are you at the Raven

Academy? No one seems to know what you do here. You're not a professor."

"Hell no." He skimmed his hand up my side, under my tank top.

I arched into him. It felt like my body had been asleep and was waking under his touch. "An administrator?"

He snorted. "Does it look like I do paperwork?"

Not unless I changed my name to 'paperwork.' I threw out a last-ditch guess. "Janitor?"

His hand stopped roaming. He rocked back onto his knees. "What's with all the questions?"

I lifted a shoulder. "Call it an odd quirk of mine, but I do like to know a little about the man I'm about to sleep with. You can ask me whatever you want, too."

"I already know everything I need to about you."

"Oh yeah?"

"Yeah." He drew a circle around my nipple over my shirt. "I know you don't want to be the Chosen One. That you'll risk your life to save your friends. And I know no matter how hard you get knocked down, you always get back up." He planted his hands on either side of my head, leaning down till we were nose to nose. "I know everything that matters."

I didn't know if I liked that all he saw were my good parts or was annoyed that he didn't want to look deeper, to get to know my flaws. Though not wanting to be the stupid Chosen One was probably a flaw in his book. He'd probably jump at the chance to save the world.

*Or destroy it*. I couldn't forget that the prophecy was a wee bit ambiguous on that point.

Well, he might know all he wanted about me, but I, however, needed more.

"I saw you talking to one of the council members when they arrived after we defeated Thanness," I said. "Are you..." I was talking to air. I blinked, and he was gone. I pushed up to sitting and looked around. "Gareth?"

"Here."

I swung my head to the back wall. Gareth wiped the shaft of a sai we'd fought with before hanging it on his wall of weapons. Or as I like to call it, the wall of awesomeness. "I don't think we're going to get any more training in today," he said. "I'll see you tomorrow."

"What?" I wrapped my arms around my knees, feeling a chill wrap around me. The dismissal in his voice was clear, but I didn't understand it. How did he go from groping me on the floor, telling me how great I was, to wanting me gone?

"We're done for today." He turned his back, picked out another weapon to clean.

I got to my feet. Had I thought his kisses felt familiar? I was much more accustomed to this. The feeling of someone wanting me gone. Of not being wanted. This was as familiar to me as my favorite pair of jeans.

"Done for the day or we're just done?" I was impressed by how cool my voice sounded, as though his answer didn't matter. That his answer wouldn't gut me. But I'd had practice pretending indifference. It was a lesson I'd learned early in life. I'd hoped my life at the academy would be different.

He turned. "Done for the day. I told you before this isn't over between us, and I meant it. But there are things I can't talk about. Don't push."

"I just want to know you better."

"How well does anyone truly know another?" Gareth clenched his hand. "Good night, Delaney. Sweet dreams."

I kept my pace even until I got through his door. Until I was alone under the night sky. Then I stumbled forward, wanting to get as much distance as I could.

He didn't owe me anything. Not answers, not his life story. I knew this.

But still it hurt. Almost enough to make me turn and give the shadow tailing me back to the academy a piece of my mind. Because even though Gareth had dismissed me, of course, he followed me as I walked back home. Of course, he'd make sure I didn't have another run-in with those minges. That was just the type of demon he was. Protective, even when pushing me away.

When I did climb into bed, I hoped for the first time since I'd arrived at the academy that I wouldn't dream of any of my men tonight. I didn't know if my heart could take it.

# Chapter Seven

His elbow patch disappeared around the corner, and I sprinted on my tiptoes to the bend in the corridor before peering around it.

Professor Bane had his head down, reading papers in his hand as he strode toward his office. My gaze trailed from his wide, tweed-covered shoulders down to his completely bitable ass.

I jerked my eyes up. *Focus.* I was on a mission here.

It had been a couple of days since I'd found Dante hanging from his heels. Nothing else had happened to him, so maybe he was right that it had been nothing but a prank. My nightly training sessions had continued with Gareth, but there'd been no repeats of our groping session.

And I was bored out of my ever-loving mind.

Aside from keeping a look-out for Ophelia and any attacks she might launch—I snuck another glance around the hallway for her as I slunk next to the wall—I had nothing to do. Dante was still in research hell reading through all the data we'd stolen. So I'd decided to track down Bane and see if he had any new intel.

But sneaky-like. To impress him with my ninja-like tracking skills.

Like I said, I was bored. I mean, I guess I could study more, but come on. That just wasn't going to happen. Besides, I learned so much more from my training sessions than I ever would from a book.

He pushed through his office door and knocked it closed with his heel, the door easing shut over the thin carpet.

Darting forward, I slid sideways through the narrowing gap and pressed my back against his wall.

He stood in front of his desk, still reading, and I couldn't wait for him to turn, to start in surprise.

"Good morning, Miss Jones. Something I can do for you?"

I sucked in a breath. "How did you—?" I shoved my arms across my chest. "Do you have eyes on the back of your head?"

"Sadly, I do not." He tossed his sheaf of papers down and turned, cocking his hip on the edge of the desk. "Is there a reason you were tiptoeing as unobtrusively as an elephant after me? Or is this just my lucky day?"

I pushed off the wall and stalked forward. He didn't move so I had to brush against him as I took the seat in front of his desk.

Which gave me an eye-level view of his crotch.

I squeezed my thighs together. Probably not the best thing for me to look at as I held a conversation. Way too distracting. I jerked my gaze up to his face, my own heating. "Um, I was wondering if you have any new information? Any new places we should break into? Anyone to fight?" I asked hopefully.

He arched a dark brow. "Feeling restless, are we?"

I huffed. "I don't know how *you* feel, but I would willingly wrestle an alligator right about now." To make matters worse, my dreams *had* stopped. I'd wanted a one-night reprieve from them but it had been three nights now. Three nights without feeling the touch of any of my guys. Even the weird dream where they all chanted around me would be welcome at this point. At least I was the center of their attention in it.

And I knew that was pathetic, both my desire to be the center of their attention and that a dream had fulfilled that for me in part. But, damn it, Dante was buried in his computer, Gareth was monosyllabic and hands-off, and Bane...

Well, Bane was Bane. Ignoring me. Trying to keep professional boundaries.

It was all enough to make me want to shimmy on my hot pants again and climb in the ring.

My lungs froze. Oh shit. Was that why I fought?

Was I an attention slut?

Bane grabbed my shoulder. "Are you all right? Your face went a bit green there for a moment."

I plastered on a bright smile. Uncomfortable self-realizations could wait until... never. "I'm fine. But seriously, I need something to do."

He frowned. "You're supposed to be improving your magic."

"Besides that." I bobbed my foot. "What about that prophecy? You read it to me, but there has to be more to it. Maybe I can research the witch who made it, maybe even find her—"

"She's dead." Bane scrubbed a hand across his jaw. He had the barest hint of stubble, and my fingers itched to feel that slight bit of roughness against them. I shifted in my seat. Or to feel that nip of abrasion somewhere else. Like against the soft skin of my thighs as he went down on me, my fingers threaded through his dark hair, holding him tight to my body, never letting him get away....

My mouth went dry. I'd been up close and personal with Dante and Gareth—*very* personal with Dante—but I'd yet to feel anything from Bane other than his hand on mine. And my body ached to get close.

"Want me to give you a haircut?"

"What?" The skin between his eyebrows pinched in confusion.

"Nothing." Jesus, I really needed something to do. And from the look on Bane's face, it wouldn't be a replay of Paulina Porizkova cutting Tom Selleck's hair in *Her Alibi*. God, I loved cheesy eighties movies.

Maybe I'd do a movie marathon. Hazel and Quincy would probably be down for that.

"Are you sure you're all right?" He looked me up and down, his gaze as clinical as a doctor's. "Minge attacks shouldn't have lasting effects, but you are looking a bit peaked."

"So you know about that." I'd debated whether to tell him. But of all my men, I worried most about Bane getting frustrated by the attacks and locking me away somewhere.

I wouldn't do well in lockdown. I needed people. Action. Lime-flavored tortilla chips.

I eyed the neat knot in Bane's tie. He didn't seem like the type to indulge my noshing habits.

And in the back of my mind I guess I knew Gareth would spill the beans for me anyway.

"Of course I know about it." He narrowed his eyes. "The breach in our wards is being investigated."

"Do you think someone was trying to kill me?" Could those bugs be trained to attack on command?

"Unlikely. Raven's security has become a bit lax. We've had so much turnover in staff that some things have fallen through the cracks."

I nodded. Sometimes shit did just happen. Not everything was about me. Even though the timing still seemed awfully suspicious.

"What do you know of your parents' lineage?" Bane asked.

My eyebrows squished together. "Uh, non sequitur much?"

He gave me a small smile, and I knew I'd got that Latin term right. I stopped myself from offering my hand up for a high five. Bane would probably leave me hanging.

"There are two parts to any prophecy," he said. "The one who makes it, and the one whom it is made about. Druella Bancroft was an esteemed witch. She wrote two biographies and won multiple awards. We know just about everything there is to know about her. You, however, are more of a mystery."

I shrugged. "You already know the highlights. Mom died when I was five. She must have been a witch, but I don't think my dad knew. Magic was just something in movies when I was growing up."

He stared at me a moment, then rounded his desk and pulled open the bottom drawer. He removed a manila file folder and came back around to stand in front of me. "Your mother *was* a witch. From a renowned family. It's your father I can't find any information on."

"You're researching my parents?" It made sense. I could be the destroyer of worlds after all. But it still left me with a sick feeling in my stomach. It was an invasion of privacy, and I wondered how many background checks he'd made on me.

He held out the folder. "It's what I know of your mother."

I reached for it, but he held on, keeping us connected.

"A prophecy of this magnitude isn't likely to be made about a half-blood witch." He frowned. "Anything you can tell me about your father—"

I snorted. "My dad doesn't have a magical bone in his body, you can trust me on that. Another reason to suspect I'm not the Chosen One." I tugged, and this time he let go.

"Nevertheless," he began, "I..." He swung his head from left to right. Sniffed. "Do you smell that?"

"No, but I've been a little stuffed—"

"Smoke!"

I jumped to my feet, bringing me dangerously close to Bane. My breasts brushed his chest, and he inhaled sharply.

"Do you still smell it? Is there a fire?" I didn't see any smoke. Felt no heat except from Bane's body.

"What?"

I glanced up. His eyes were closed. His jaw tight. And when he inhaled this time, he leaned down the slightest bit, as if he was inhaling me.

"Does my hair smell like smoke?"

"No." He cleared his throat. "I need to investigate. Stay here." He set me aside and strode to his door, pausing to feel the wood.

I rolled my eyes and followed when he left. Really, he knew better than to say something so stupid like for me to stay put.

The scent grew stronger when we reached the lower level. Students spilled into the great hall, coughing, with streaks of ash coating their clothes and faces. Tendrils of smoke followed them from the cafeteria.

And like a fool hero, Bane pushed through the students and rushed into the fire.

And like the bigger idiot, I followed.

Inside the cafeteria, it was chaos. Someone had been smart enough to open the windows that lined two walls and my eyes only stung a little as I looked around, trying to make sense of it.

A guy was curled up under one of the tables, his shoulders shaking. Another student sat in the corner, rocking back and forth, her eyes wide and glassy. Ophelia and her squad sat at their usual table, smirking and laughing. The cook and kitchen staff were spraying one wall with both fire extinguishers and water that magically spouted from their hands. And one very confused looking girl stood in the center of the cafeteria, her face blackened with soot and smoke.

Ophelia caught sight of me and jumped from her seat. We squared off, hands twitching at our sides. It felt like a scene from a Western, each of us waiting for the other to draw. Or strike magically as the case might be.

Another group of students rushed out of the cafeteria, getting between me and Ophelia. When my field of vision cleared, Ophelia was back in her chair, keeping a wary eye in my direction, but not looking like any assault was imminent. The knots in my shoulders eased.

Bane grabbed one of the fleeing students. "What happened here?"

The guy shrugged. "Xerxes won the contest."

"Oh, shit," I muttered, understanding.

""Yes, Miss Jones?" Bane ran a hand through his hair. "You can provide further clarification?"

"It's our C and D class. We were partnered up and told to launch a surprise magical attack on our opponent." I blew out a breath. "It's like our final or something."

A tiny muscle ticked in Bane's jaw. "I see. I'll have to speak with Professor Klingor about this."

Well, that would be awesome. If Bane could get this stupid test called off it would make my life exponentially easier. Although the idea of lighting Ophelia up like a Christmas tree did hold some appeal, it was exhausting watching my back all the time. And I still hadn't thought of a good spell to launch at her.

Something hard and sharp knocked into my back, sending me to my knees. The folder in my hand went flying, the documents detailing my mother's life spilling across the linoleum floor. I caught a glimpse of her smiling face in a five by seven photo just as a thick black boot came down across it.

"Hey!" I scuttled forward and pushed at the boot. "Get off my mom."

"That's not what she said last night." Obnoxious snickers followed that lame-ass joke, and I looked up the leg to the asshole who still hadn't moved.

And I blinked. Had I hit my head when I fell. Because standing above me were three identical faces under caps of dirty-blond hair. Three identical sets of ice-blue eyes. Three identical smirks.

Bane was there in an instant, getting in the face of the joker. "Move." His voice was ice. It should have chilled me to the core. Instead, it fired my blood.

"Yes, sir, professor, sir." The asshole saluted Bane, gave me a wink, and turned with his brothers and sauntered away.

Leaving a dirty imprint of his tread pattern across my mom's face.

I picked her picture up, blinking back pointless tears. Scrambling on my hands and knees, I gathered up the rest of the documents.

Bane dropped beside me. He was on his knees, probably putting a wrinkle in those creased trousers of his, and the pressure behind my eyes increased.

"Here you are, Miss Jones." He put the last piece of paper in the folder and held out his hand. "Can I see the photo?"

I'd never seen this picture before, and suddenly I didn't want to give it away, not even for a moment. But I was being stupid, so I sucked it up and gave Bane the photo.

He chanted under his breath and ran his hand over the image. When he gave it back to me, all the dirt was gone.

"Thank you," I whispered.

"Not a problem." I thought he was going to say more. He looked like he wanted to say more. But he merely stood and nodded at me, his expression back to its normally snooty state. "Good day, Miss Jones. Be sure not to miss any sessions with Gareth." And he turned on his heel and was gone.

I pushed to my feet, sliding the picture into the folder and holding it against my chest. A loud snicker of laughter drew my gaze to Ophelia's table.

And the three identical brothers who now sat around her like pages at the feet of a queen. One of the triplets turned his head, caught me in his icy stare, and a shiver coursed through me.

There was nothing friendly in that stare. Whoever these new students were, I knew they were going to be nothing but trouble.

# Chapter Eight

*Bane*

I needed out. I needed distance. Distance from *her.*

I clenched my hands.

I needed to beat some heads in.

I slammed my office door behind me, the small amount of violence nowhere near good enough to assuage the anger coursing through me.

I wanted to rip the heads from those bullies. From anyone who dared hurt her. I wanted to go track down her asshole father and teach him the proper way to raise a daughter.

But I was a professor at the academy and she a student. There was about ten years and two thousand secrets separating Delaney and I. Defending her against hurt wasn't my job.

Nor my privilege. I hadn't earned the right.

My research into the father was thin, but I'd found enough to know the neglect he'd shown Delaney. The disregard. He'd let his fifteen-year-old daughter walk out of his home to be on her own. To live on the streets for a three-month period that I didn't even want to think about before she'd been able to rent a room in a run-down house.

Her father deserved a beating, and by God, I wanted to be the one to deliver it.

Everything I'd learned about Delaney showed nothing but a short life of want and hardship. And every damn time I saw her she still gave me the sunniest damn smile I'd ever seen. I actually ached inside when I saw it.

She got up each morning, eager to figure out what was going on with the prophecy, optimistic as hell that we could defeat any trouble. She continued training with Gareth even though from the sessions I'd observed she spent most of the time getting knocked on her arse. She even kept dying her hair those absurd colors, the new deep blue a color my cock seemed to find exceptionally appealing.

She was a fighter. A survivor. And she made it look easy. Like even though the world might be ending, she was still having fun and life was good.

Which made the times when she got worn down even harder to see.

I scrubbed my hand across my jaw.

Jesus Christ, the look on her face when that punk had stepped on her mom's photo. It was almost enough to make me want to break my rules about professional conduct, gather her close, give her the comfort she needed.

Kiss the tears from her eyes, then kiss her lips until she forgot anyone who'd hurt her in the past. Slide balls-deep inside her until she forgot the future she faced. Fuck her until she forgot everything but me.

My heart lurched. It was no use dreaming of what could never be. I was a professor; she was a student.

More than that... I planted my palms on my desk and dropped my head. If she was the Chosen One... And if the prophecy foretold her destroying the world instead of saving it...

I unlocked the bottom drawer of my desk and pulled out a black velvet sack. I made sure my door was locked and my window cracked before getting to work.

I pulled a cushion from my sofa and tossed it on the ground, placing a wide silver bowl before it. I dampened a bundle of sage, ensuring it would smoke properly, before dropping it into the bowl along with two scoops of frankincense. I sat cross-legged on the cushion and lit the sage on fire.

I took cleansing breaths, letting my anger and worry drift away. I needed a clear mind for divination, and thoughts of Delaney had a tendency to cloud it.

The smoke rose, shifted. I made my eyes unfocus. I concentrated on the future. On Delaney. Was she the savior, or the destroyer, of us all?

The smoke thickened. Shapes swirled in its depths. My head went light, and I let the vision take control.

Something was moving. Writhing. There was a flash of color. Purple. Delaney's hair. She'd changed it yet again. Her face came into focus. Her cheeks were flushed, her eyes closed. Her mouth was open in what could have been a moan or a sigh.

And she was laying on a white-sheeted bed.

Naked.

I shook my head. Jesus. Not the information I was bloody looking for. And I didn't need that image in my mind. Not now. Not ever.

I refocused. *What is Delaney's role in the coming war?*

A swath of gray smoke covered her body, and I relaxed. I was an instructor of divination. I could damn well do a simple smoke scry. Except nothing about this was simple. No matter how many times I resorted to divination, the future was blocked. Shrouded in fog. But I had to try. Every damn day I had to try.

The smoke thinned. The bed had changed, red satin sheets now, but Delaney remained the same. Beautiful. Vibrant. And completely out of my grasp.

The bed dipped, and a male figure entered the scene. I clenched my hands. Rider. Her lover. That punk had already tasted her lips. Had slid into her sweet body. Was I to watch them shagging in my visions now, too?

The bed dipped on her other side, and Gareth's tattooed arse crawled close. He stroked his dark hand over her fair stomach, going lower, lower...

Sod it all to hell. I squeezed my eyes tight and shook my head. *Focus.* I wasn't interested in Delaney's nocturnal habits. I wasn't. And if I told myself that enough times, I might eventually believe it.

I called upon all my concentration. Drew my intention into my core. *Will Delaney be a force for good?*

Smoke burned the back of my throat, but I pushed the discomfort aside. I could do this. I needed to do this.

She appeared again, both men still laying by her sides. I groaned. Rider had his mouth around one of her nipples. Gareth gripped the inside of her thigh, tugging her leg wide.

And a third figure crawled between her spread legs.

I sucked in a sharp breath even as my cock throbbed. It... couldn't be. I would never...

But the dark head that bent to taste her was indeed mine. The shoulders with the magical burn scarring the right blade belonged to no one else.

"Fuck me," I whispered. I could taste her spicy nectar. I felt each lap of future-me's tongue against her soft folds. Delaney grabbed my hair in the vision, and I swore I could feel every delicious tug to my own scalp.

"Delaney." I groaned. I needed to stop this. Clear the smoke from my room. From my head. But I watched as I slid up her body. As I took her hands and pinned them to the mattress above her head. Watched as I notched my cock at her entrance and pressed—

"No!" I scrabbled backwards, my foot catching the bowl and knocking it over. My chest heaved and the front of my boxers was damp with my precum.

I pressed my palm to my erection. Jesus. Fuck. Hell. I should turn in my teaching credentials. Because there was no way that vision would come true. That wasn't the future. And it had nothing to do with my question about whether Delaney would fight for the side of good or for evil.

I cleaned up the sage and frankincense. Aired out my office. And refocused on my duty.

If Delaney was the destroyer, well, I knew what I had to do. And I couldn't do it if she meant something more to me than a student.

I couldn't make love to a woman and then turn around and take her life. I was a bastard, but not that big of one.

The security of the world was more important than my lust. Than my feelings.

And it was more important than any one life.

Even hers.

# Chapter Nine

*Delaney*

"Glad you could finally join us?" I added a smile to my words, making them a joke, but I couldn't deny my snark held a bit of truth. I'd missed Dante's presence in our classes. Ever since the battle with Thanness, his attendance had been sporadic to say the least.

Fatigue etched the corners of his chocolate eyes. He scrubbed a hand across his jaw as he dropped his satchel on the desk we shared in Potions class. "Yeah, I couldn't take another hour of reading through academy records. I needed a break."

"And you came to class to relax?" No one could like school that much.

One edge of his lip quirked up. "I came to see you. You're better than a shot of whisky."

Aww... The words were corny, but I guess I liked corny, because they did funny things to my heart. Weird, fluttering things.

One of the triplets turned and looked back at us. It wasn't a glare. It wasn't a hello, or a shut-the-fuck-up kind of look. It was flat. Emotionless. And creepy as hell.

Hazel and Quincy bustled up to our desk and stood across from us. "Hey. Professor Dram said he's a little short on supplies so we get to double up with you guys today." She plopped a wooden box in the center of the high table. "Our ingredients for today's potion."

"Great." My word said one thing, my voice something else. Potions was one of my least favorite classes. I'd almost been blown up the first time I used a cauldron, and the memory lingered. True, that had been in Herbology, but I'd been making a poultice and that was very potion-like.

Potions also required more precision than I liked. The formulas needed complete accuracy in order to make a successful brew, and I was more of a fly-by-the-seat-of-your-pants kind of gal. It was like cooking versus baking. Baking needed exact measurements or your cake caved. Cooking you could just toss stuff in a pan and wing it.

Sadly, I couldn't bake worth shit.

Quincy shot me a sympathetic look.

Hazel unpacked the ingredients from the box, humming under her breath.

She was a baker.

I leaned forward, planting my elbows on the desk. "Hey, does anyone know those guys' stories?" I nodded to the triplets. Two were at one table and the third had paired up with Ophelia. Her old partner had been banished to an empty desk across the room, and the girl shot longing looks back at the cool crowd.

"The Beautiful Bastards?" Hazel raised her eyebrow. "I hear they were sent here as punishment for seducing the Duchess of Morag. And then stealing her tiara. It was either the Raven Academy or magic jail for them."

There was a lot to unpack in that statement. "Who's the Duchess of Morag? Is that part of the British royalty?"

Dante huffed out a laugh. "Morag is a duchy in the lower world. Lucifer is a pretentious git and set up a royalty system down in hell."

"Okay," I said slowly, trying to keep my face impassive. I felt like a hillbilly in a palace and didn't want to showcase my ignorance. But Lucifer was real? And hell? I really needed to get back into confession. The last time I'd been in church I'd been six years old, but it was never too late to get on God's good side. I hoped.

"The triplets just got here," I said. "They're already known a-holes?"

Hazel frowned, her widow's peak dipping low. "What? Oh, because of the bastard bit. No." She lit the Bunsen burner at the center of our desk and placed the mini-cauldron on the stand over it. "No, they're Bastardo's. Of the famed Bastardo's?"

I shrugged.

"It was chapter one in our history of magic textbook?" Hazel waved her hand. "No matter. Morgana Ravencroft's sister married into the Bastardo's. They gave her some money to start the academy, so, in essence, they were founders of Raven, too. Which explains why the three delinquents were allowed in mid-term. Legacy admissions." She snorted.

I examined the three blonds. What Hazel said made sense. They were probably nothing but trouble makers with rich, connected parents that had forced them here. They sure acted like entitled pricks.

But I was wary of any new faces. I was going to keep a sharp eye on the trio. "Do you know their names?"

"Braxton, Boaz, and Brinlee," Dante answered. "Their parents sure went with the B theme," he said dryly.

"And they're distantly related to Ophelia." I watched as the girl in question leaned into the brother by her side, smiling demurely up at him. "Distant enough where it wouldn't be weird if she screwed them?"

Quincy choked on his saliva and started coughing.

Hazel pounded him on the back. "Uh, screwing any three guys would be weird."

My cheeks flamed, and I could feel Dante's gaze on me like it was a brand. "Screwing three brothers would be weird." But if it was my three guys... A pulse throbbed in my core. Yeah, maybe that would still be weird. But it didn't feel like it. It felt like it could be wonderful.

I just needed to work the logistics out. If it wasn't one after the other like in my dreams, I could have Dante in my mouth, Gareth—

Nah, still weird. And there was no way Gareth would watch me touch another man. None of my men seemed like the sharing type.

Dante nudged my side with his elbow. "Earth to Delaney. You okay there, babe?"

His mouth was even, but his eyes crinkled around the edges. The bastard knew. Knew what he did to me. Knew what Gareth and Bane did to me, too. He knew and apparently found it amusing as hell.

"I'm fine." I pulled the Potions book toward me and looked at the spell we'd be creating today: a Euphoria Elixir. "Let's get this done."

And we did. Nothing blew up on us—huzzah!—it smoked the lovely lime green color it was supposed to, and when the professor came around and Quincy tested our work product, we received a 'nicely done' from Professor Dram as a goofy smile creased our friend's face.

When class ended, Hazel broke out ahead of us, slipping out the door before the rest of us had gathered our bags.

A high-pitched scream echoed from the hallway.

We all looked at each other before racing out. Only to find Hazel blowing on her fingertips and a horrified member of Ophelia's squad, Rosamunde, quivering before her.

Quivering and purple.

"What the hell?" I sidled around the spelled girl to get to Hazel. "Did you do that?"

"Yep." She pulled out her phone and snapped a pic of Rosamunde. "Consider my C and D class aced."

I looked at my friend. Looked at Rosamunde. Every inch of her skin was a deep purple, even her nails. With her blond hair and light eyes, it was rather a striking effect.

Rosamunde didn't seem to think so. "Take it off!" she wailed. She flipped her hands over and back, as though hoping to see something different each time she looked at her palms.

"It'll wear off. In a couple days." Hazel smirked. "Come on, Quincy. Let's get some grub."

Still under the effects of the euphoria draught, Quincy tripped after her, humming under his breath.

But me? I had a whole new respect for my friend. And a little bit of fear. But mostly respect. Spelling someone to turn purple might not have any self-defense applications, but it was funny as hell. And something she was going to have to teach me.

Dante threw his arm around my shoulders. "Grub sounds good. Let's go have dinner."

"Okay." We left Rosamunde still wailing, surrounded by her snickering friends. "Uh, the cafeteria is that way," I said, pointing as he led us in the wrong direction.

"We're not eating dinner in the cafeteria."

I bobbed on my toes. "Ooh, are you taking me to the Quarter?"

He cleared his throat. "Uh, no. Sorry. I had something else in mind."

The tips of his ears were red, and my suspicious mind when on immediate alert.

Dante was up to something.

And I couldn't wait to find out what.

# Chapter Ten

I followed Dante up the stairs toward his room. I couldn't deny the small kernel of disappointment wedged in my gut. I'd heard such amazing things about the restaurants in New Orleans. It would have been nice to try one out. And fun to sneak out of the academy again.

But when Dante opened the door to his room, any disappointment I was feeling evaporated.

His desk had been cleared and moved to the center of the room. A white tablecloth was draped over it, one edge skimming the floor. Two thick candles stood on either end of the make-shift table, what looked like real china made up two place settings, and a covered platter was notched in the corner.

"You did this?" I dropped my messenger bag and breathed in the scents of... I sniffed again, my mouth watering. Rosemary and chicken.

He nodded. With a flick of his wrist, the candles burst to life. Dante turned off the lights, letting the burgeoning twilight and the candles do all the work. "Do you like it?"

I spun and threw my arms around his neck. "I love it!" And I did. No one had ever done anything like this for me. My best date had been chicken fingers at T.G.I. Fridays. Don't get me wrong, their chicken fingers are awesome. But they couldn't compare to a candlelit dinner with a man I was coming to lo— care greatly about.

He slid his hands down my waist and gripped my hips. "I'm glad. And you don't have to worry about the food. I had cook make up something special."

"I would have eaten anything you made." But since my nose was doing a happy dance at the scents coming from that covered tray, this was probably for the best. I let him take my jacket and pull out my chair, enjoying the feeling of being taken care of. "Why did you do this?" I asked as he sat across from me.

"I wasn't lying when I said I needed a break." He waggled his eyebrows. "I was hoping you could find several inventive ways to relax me."

"And those ways need us to be alone in a room together?" I teased.

"Most definitely." He pulled a bottle of wine from under the table and poured us each a glass. "Unless you like being watched. Then I'd try to make that work, too."

My glass froze at my lips. He wasn't serious. He couldn't be. But as I took a sip and the velvety smoothness of the ruby liquid slid over my tongue, I couldn't help but think, what if?

What if he was serious? I knew Dante wanted me. And he knew I also had feelings for Gareth and Bane. Was he offering... to share?

When he placed a juicy breast on my plate, I impaled the poor chicken with my fork. Why was this so confusing? And why did I worry more about my relationships than I did about the possible end of the world? My priorities were seriously messed up.

"Whoa," Dante said with a smile. "What did that poor chicken ever do to you?"

I smiled. "Nothing. This is amazing. Thank you so much, Dante. No one's ever done anything like this for me before."

His eyes darkened. "I can't say I'm not happy to be the first to wine and dine you, but someone should have done this for you long ago. You deserve so much, Delaney. Deserve to be treated like a queen."

A queen? I placed a bite of the buttery chicken in my mouth and hummed happily. I'd be happy mucking the queen's stables as long as I got to eat from the castle's kitchen.

I took another sip of wine. "I think court jester suits me better." I winked. "I can't imagine people lining up to worship me."

"Why do you do that?" He laid his silverware down and placed his elbows on the table. "Why do you put yourself down?"

"I..." I had no answer to that. So I pushed my chicken and vegetables around on my plate. I didn't think I had self-esteem issues. For the most part, I thought I was pretty awesome. But sincere compliments did make me uncomfortable. The truth was, it was easier to dismiss my worth than wait for someone else to do it. Easier on the heart, too.

His hand covered mine, warm and solid. "It's okay to acknowledge what an amazing woman you are. To flaunt it even sometimes."

I stared at his hand. At the fine hairs that sprinkled the backs of his knuckles. At the small scar that crossed his right middle finger.

*You're nothing special, kid. Who would ever want a train wreck like you?*

The voice in my brain was one I hadn't heard in years. One I'd hoped to never hear again.

But one that I'd believed. If I wasn't possibly this Chosen One. If I didn't have people after me, trying to kill me. Would I have even caught the eye of Dante? Of Gareth and Bane? It was the circumstances, the whole damsel-in-distress thing that snagged their attention. I made a pretty impressive human, but as a witch, everyone knew I was subpar. Including my guys.

But thoughts like those were useless. So I shrugged them off and made another joke. "Hey, I named myself Giantslayer Jones. I know I rock. And I won't let any of you forget it, either."

The smile he gave me was tighter than I was used to. A little smaller. Like he was disappointed in me.

I shrugged that off, too.

"This is really good." I forked up another bite. "I can't wait to see what you got for dessert."

At that, his smile went full wide. "You're insatiable. Or at least, that's what I was hoping." His knee brushed against my thigh. His eyes were hot as he watched me slide the food off my fork, lick it clean.

"You keep feeding me like this, I'll let you do whatever you want," I teased.

"Good to know."

It was silent a moment as we both focused on our meals. When I cleaned my plate, I asked, "Have there been any more—"

"No." He blew out a breath. "No more hanging upside-down episodes. You really need to forget about it."

"Okay." I picked up my glass and stared into my wine. "It's not like I don't have other things to worry about."

"What's going on? Until I finish going through all the files, we can't do anything about the prophecy."

"The stupid prophecy isn't my only problem."

He nudged my leg. "So? What is?"

I finished my wine and waved him off when he went to refill it. "I don't think it's anything you want to hear about."

"I want to know everything about you. Tell me." There was a seriousness in his voice I hadn't heard before. So I decided to give it a shot.

"It's about Gareth." I paused, giving him time to object to the conversational topic. No guy wanted to hear about his rival.

His eyes narrowed a little, but he nodded. "Go on."

"He's keeping something from me." I twisted my ring around my thumb. "We were... well I asked him to tell me a bit about himself, and he completely shut down. Basically said it wasn't my business. Which in one respect, yeah, okay, he's right. But in another, we've fought together. Are planning on saving the world together. I don't think it's unreasonable that he tells me a bit more about who he is."

Dante clasped his hands together and rested them at the back of his head. His T-shirt pulled tight across his chest, and I almost missed his words as my ogling took precedence. "He's a private guy. A demon. Maybe you don't want to know those secrets."

"If he expects us to have any sort of relationship moving forward, I'd better damn well learn a couple of those secrets."

Dante winced at the word relationship.

"Sorry," I said. But he'd asked. And I was on a roll now. "I hate that he won't tell me about himself. I hate secrets. If he were human, at least I'd have a known spread of possibilities. A girlfriend stashed away somewhere. A hidden kink for chocolate syrup. But he's a demon. I have no idea what sort of secrets demons might keep. Does he like eating babies? Drinking blood? The possibilities are endless. I won't be in a relationship with someone who keeps secrets from me. I just won't do it."

Dante swallowed, his face gone pale.

"Are you okay?" I leaned forward and pressed my palm to his forehead. "Was it the chicken?"

"I'm fine." He took my hand from his head but didn't let it go. He gently massaged it as he stared down at the table. "It sounds like this is a deal breaker for you."

"It is." I got up and circled the table, stretching to keep my hand in his. It was such a small part of my body, but the hand massage felt amazing. I didn't want him to stop. I nudged the table back a couple of inches and dropped into his lap. "But enough about Gareth. Although..." I checked the clock in his room. "I do have to get to his gym in twenty minutes." I turned my attention back to Dante. "But we could make the most of those twenty minutes."

His cock hardened beneath my butt. My clit pulsed in anticipation. I felt so empty, and I couldn't wait to have Dante fill me again. Couldn't wait to spread my legs and sink down on—

Dante picked me up and deposited me next to his chair.

I blinked. "Uh, what? What just happened?" We were having a nice moment; I was grinding against his cock. What would make him want to stop that?

"Nothing." He wiped his mouth with his napkin and stood. "It's just time for you to get to Gareth's. I don't want you to be late to training on my account."

"Yeah." I chewed on my bottom lip. "Okay." That sounded totally plausible. That a guy would give up some nooky just so I wasn't late to the gym.

*Not.*

"Are you mad at me for something?"

He tugged on my ponytail, a warm smile creasing his face. "I'm not mad. Look, I'll walk you to Gareth's."

We left the dirty plates on his table, my favorite place to leave dinner plates, and strolled out of the main building and across the woods to Gareth's cottage. I let my fingers brush against Dante's several times, but he never picked up the hint and took my hand.

He opened the door for me, letting me enter before him.

Then shoved me hard in the back, making me stumble to my knees.

A bright flare of blue lightning streaked past my shoulder, knocking the door off its hinges.

I twisted, looking for the source.

And there, not ten feet away, stood Gareth. Another orb of electricity still hovered over his open palm.

And one pissed off expression lined the demon's face.

# Chapter Eleven

"What are you doing here?" Gareth growled, stalking toward Dante.

Dante threw out his hands, and the demon bounced off an invisible wall. "Obviously protecting Delaney from you. What the hell, man? What's got into you?"

The tattoos on Gareth's arms and neck swirled dizzyingly fast. He raised one hand, and his nails extended into claws. He swiped through the magical barrier, his claws dragging on invisible threads. "This is my training time with her. You don't belong here."

I rolled to my feet and jumped between them. I could sense when a situation could go downhill fast, and this had the potential of avalanche-level proportions.

"Whoa!" I held up my hands. "Everyone, calm down." I turned to Dante. "This is what he does. He doesn't always wait for me to prepare to defend myself." A fact that had landed me on my ass more times than I wanted to remember. Even with all the padding I had back there, my butt was still bruised from these sessions.

Dante's shoulders lowered an inch. "This is your training? The demon trying to take your head off?"

"Hey!" I scowled, fisting my hands on my hips. "I can defend against his attacks." Sort of. But Dante didn't need to know that.

Gareth sauntered next to me and dropped his arm over my shoulder.

I staggered.

"Delaney can take care of herself." He made a shooing motion with his other hand. "Away with you, pup. Your chivalry isn't needed."

Dante bared his teeth. "I'll always be there for her. Standing right behind her whenever she needs me."

"Behind Delaney?" Gareth bent and inhaled deeply, smelling my hair. "That's my position. You'll have to find your own."

"Oh, good lord," I muttered. I shrugged out from under Gareth's arm. "Can we just get started? Or do you two want to pull out your dicks and measure them right here?"

Gareth tipped his head to the side, pursing those full lips.

I smacked his stomach. "No. Now let's get going." I pointed at Dante. "You can stay, but only if you stay in the side-lines. No interfering." I tightened my hair band and marched to the center of the mats.

These guys were as irritating as water to a cat, and it was seriously interfering with the zen I needed to gather my intention.

He didn't give me time to gather. Gareth tossed another ball of blue electricity into the air and batted it at me. Hard.

And my hands flew up, meeting the orb, and redirecting it through Gareth's window.

Whoa. I examined my palms. Maybe I didn't need zen.

Dante lounged against the far wall. "I told you your power comes from your emotion. You're an elemental. High emotions power you."

"You told Bane that, not me." But Dante might be onto something. Bane had trained in a system of magic that relied on will and intention alone. It's what was taught at the academy.

But maybe I did magic in a different way. Maybe I needed to learn in a different way.

Excitement rushed through my veins. I might become a good witch after all.

A draft of cool air teased my bare arms. I looked to the broken window and grimaced. "Sorry about your wind—"

The blast took me by surprise. I threw up my hands, but no power surged through them. Instead, the bolt hit me square in the chest, rocketing me back ten feet.

"Son of a beehive." I stomped to my feet. I pointed at Dante. "You. Piss me off again."

He frowned. "Again? When did I piss you off the first time?"

Men. So clueless.

I didn't have time to argue. Gareth threw another bolt of magic at me. I leapt to the side, doing a modified side roll. My center swelled with all the intention in the world to knock Gareth on his ass, but all that came out of my hands was a limp little red sparkle.

Gareth watched the meandering bit of magic as it approached, not even bothering to block it. He just let the sparkles hit his chest, gave a little shrug, and lifted his eyes to me with a 'that's it?' kind of expression.

Bugger. Not only did my magic come from emotion, it seemed to come from anger, and I never stayed angry for long. I'd thought that was a good thing. Until now.

I popped to my feet and sprinted for his wall of weapons. If my magic was puttering out, I'd go old-school. I was still a damn good fight—

Gareth blinked into appearance in front of me, smiled as I squawked and side-stepped around him, then wrapped one thick arm around my waist and took me down.

His body settled over mine. His nose was only inches from my own. He was hardly breathing, and I was panting like a banshee. Assuming banshees panted. It seemed like something they'd do, but what did I know? I'd never met one.

He tutted. "No more toys, pet. You're here for magical training."

"But..." I looked at the wall. At all the shiny metal blades. "My battle axe."

His lips twitched but he fought off his smile. Gathering my hands in one of his, he pressed my wrists into the mat above my head. "And I'll wrap it in a pretty bow and give it to you if you can use magic to get me off of you."

I tried to bring my arms down, but he only tightened his grip. "I'll need my hands."

"No, you won't." He gave me more of his weight, and I didn't know if it was his chest pressing against my lungs or his thick cock nestling against my pussy that stole my breath. Probably a combination of the two.

"Your hands are only a tool to focus your energies, but it's not a requirement that you use them for your spells." He drew the pad of his finger from my temple, down my cheek, and around my jaw.

My back arched with a delicious shiver, my thighs automatically widening. Just as my body could go on auto-pilot to fight, it seemed to need no input from my brain to fuck, either.

"Sometimes," he said, "your hands will be otherwise occupied. You need to learn how to channel your energy without them."

A strangled groan made my head swing toward the opposite wall. Dante was seated with his back against it, a look I'd never seen on his face before. Anger. Lust. Interest. Disgust. Hunger. All wrapped into one.

My hips rocked into Gareth's as my gaze stayed locked on Dante's. This was so fucking wrong.

Gareth shifted, the hard ridge of his erection rubbing against my clit.

And it felt so fucking right.

Gareth dragged his nose up my throat. When he reached my ear, he drew my lobe into his mouth, scraping his teeth along it before nipping hard enough to make me gasp.

"Should I show him how it's done?" Gareth growled. His lips brushed my neck, the patch right below my ear. There might have been some tongue involved, too. "Show him how best to make you scream? To make you come?"

Oh God. Did Dante nod? Giving his approval? It looked like he nodded. But that's what I wanted to see.

Dante had talked about letting someone else watch us, now he was the one watching.

Gareth slid his hand down my thigh and tugged it around his hip. "Your magic is powered by high emotions, it seems. I wonder how powerful you'd get when I'm buried deep inside you." He circled his hips, increasing the pressure just where I needed it.

Magic? Who cared about magic at a time like this? This had to be the hottest moment in my life and I didn't want it ruined with thoughts of magic or prophecies or the end of the world.

But a small part of myself, a stupid, selfish part that obviously didn't want me having sexy, good times, wouldn't let me just enjoy this. It had to get snarky. "Oh sure, now that Dante is here, you're hands-on again. Where was all this seduction the last couple of days?"

"Did you miss my touch, pet?"

God yes. My nipples were hard peaks, aching for his touch. His lips. I was ready to dry hump him into next year, even though he hadn't told me anything more about himself. Even though we had an audience. But I didn't tell him that. "I don't like being a pawn in a pissing match."

"Is that what you think you are?" His eyes went black, his pupils widening until I thought I could fall into them. He lowered, his lips butterflying over mine. "But there is no competition between me and the boy, is there? He's not the one you dream about at night. Not the one you picture when you slide your fingers into your sweet pussy and make yourself come."

If only he knew. Knew that I pictured all of them. Dreamed of all of them. Needed all of them. Maybe then he wouldn't be so cocky.

He slid his palm under my tank and over my ribs. He cupped my breast, brushing his thumb over my nipple.

I moaned. Then again, I didn't think anything could bruise the demon's ego. And I didn't want anything to.

His cockiness was well deserved. And if he was cool with fucking me in front of Dante, who was I to complain?

"Interesting training technique, demon." Bane's sexy accent wrapped around me, stroked me between my legs. His voice was lower than I'd ever heard. Rougher. But his expression was just as condescending as always. He stood in the doorway, arms crossed over his chest, one eyebrow arching under his dark hair.

"Sinjin," I whispered. His given name tasted good on my tongue. He'd taste better.

I didn't think it possible, but his eyebrow went even higher, his look becoming even more disapproving.

And all my warm, sexy feelings disappeared.

Gareth must have felt the change, as well. He removed his hand from my breast, the other from my wrists. He did a neat push-up off my body and got to his feet. He offered me a hand, and I gratefully took it.

I didn't know if I could sit upright let alone stand on my own. My knees didn't want to support me. But that's what training was for. Okay, not for this exact situation. But my training for the ring had taught me how to dig deep, keep going when I thought I couldn't take another step.

I locked my shaking knees, threw my shoulders back, and lifted my chin. I stood before Bane and his disdain and didn't let his disapproval affect me. Well, not much anyway.

Dante also rose, but not before adjusting himself and shooting Gareth a look that should have incinerated the demon.

I don't know what he was so pissy about. He wasn't the one who'd been revved up and then left to idle.

My gaze dropped to Dante's crotch, and the large bulge pressing against the fly of his pants.

Then again, maybe he'd earned his pissiness.

"Why are you here?" Gareth asked Bane. Gareth, on the other hand, looked as cool as ice cream. Like foreplay in front of witnesses were an everyday occurrence.

"I came to check on Miss Jones's progress." Bane shoved his hands into his jacket pockets. "Perhaps I should have been monitoring her training more closely. It doesn't seem as though any progress has been made at all. At least none magical."

I fisted my hand. "You know what? I'm done with all of you tonight." I jabbed my finger in Bane's direction. "I don't need your high-and-mighty attitude. I *am* making progress, asshole. You're just too busy to see it." I swung my hand at Gareth. "And no more of your will-he-won't-he BS. Stop playing the coy tease. And you!" I stalked forward and poked my finger into

Dante's chest. "You need to stop sending me mixed messages. I'm tired of all of you, and I want one damn night alone."

I stomped off, ignoring Gareth's deep chuckle as I sailed out his door. Of course, he wasn't insulted. Of course, he'd find my temper tantrum cute.

I stomped harder, kicking up dirt before I reached the paved path back to the academy.

I should have showed Bane some of my magic now. I was angry enough to really blast him. I hesitated. Should I go back and show him what I had?

I blew out a breath and continued on into the academy. What was the use? My anger was already waning. I'd probably only be able to show him sparkle fingers. Besides, I had a rose-scented bath waiting for me with my name on it.

I didn't know how much bath crystals and hot water could help with my current mood, but they were worth a try.

My life was about as effed up as it could get.

Or so I thought.

Because then I found the package.

# Chapter Twelve

Dante

I stalked through the empty halls of the academy. My fists clenched and unclenched, just looking for something to punch.

How dare that fucking demon put his hands on her? His lips?

I pounded a hole in the wall, but the dent in the plaster didn't cool any of my anger.

And why the fuck did I just sit there and watch?

My dick throbbed. It knew the answer. Knew how fucked up I was and didn't care. If it couldn't sink into Delaney's heat itself, well, it supposed watching someone else take her was a happy second best.

I'd never watched someone else pleasure my woman before. Didn't think it was possible without committing violence against the man. But fuck, watching Delaney's eyes glaze over in desire as the demon had touched her had been hot as hell.

I'd never participated in a three-some before, either, but if Bane hadn't walked in, that might have been where we were heading.

Something shifted, smoke-like, by a dark classroom. Professor Killough stepped out of the shadows. "Mr. Rider." He nodded, his hair shining silver in the low lights. "Do you have a moment?"

Great. A fucking vamp. Just what I didn't need. "No." I pushed past him, letting my shoulder smack into his.

He chuckled as he fell into step behind me. "Too busy punching walls?"

"What's it to you?"

"I was sent here to help you."

That made me pause. Had the white lodge taken to hiring vampires?

"Your family is very concerned," he continued.

I cracked my neck and kept on walking. "Not interested." At least that was one potential threat against

Delaney that could be eliminated. Killough wasn't here for her. She'd be relieved when I told her.

Except, I couldn't tell her. Not without revealing my secret. And that was something I wasn't ready to do.

I swallowed, the back of my throat burning. The thought of her turning away from me, the trust in her eyes transforming into disgust…

I quickened my step. Not that that was a guarantee. She let the demon touch her. Maybe she would accept me, too.

If I hadn't kept it a secret in the first place. I didn't know if she would forgive me my lies, not when honesty was so important to her.

Killough clapped a hand on my shoulder, pulling me up short, and I spun with a snarl.

"Hands off, blood-sucker." I slapped his arm away. Maybe this was a target I could beat my frustrations out on. Perhaps my family had actually done something right by me for once by sending him my way.

The vampire raised his hands, palms out. "I'm not your enemy. And I could be your friend, if you'd let me. You need me, Dante. I know it. You know it. Your family knows it."

"My *family* doesn't know shit." I circled around him. "I've been doing fine for twenty-five years now. Haven't needed you before. Don't need you now."

Killough tilted his head. "Is this because of the girl? Is that why you—"

I grabbed his throat and slammed him into the wall. "Do not talk about her. Don't even think about her."

"That will be difficult as she's one of my students." He flicked his gaze down to my arm and back up. "You know I don't need air. Choking me is pointless."

"But breaking your neck?" I squeezed harder. "Ripping your head from your body? That will do the trick."

"Have you always been this angry, Dante?" Sympathy warmed his eyes. "Or is it only since the transformation has started?"

I could see it. Could see my fingers digging into his cold flesh until I gripped his spinal column and snapped it.

But that would be something a monster would do. And I wasn't a monster.

I released my hold on him, brushed the fabric on his shoulders to release the wrinkles. "I only get angry when some asshole pisses me off. You should make sure you don't do it again." I turned and sauntered away.

"You can't stop it," Killough called after me. "You can only embrace it."

My shoulders drew back. But I kept walking. Embracing it was something I could never do.

# Chapter Thirteen

D*elaney*

It had been neatly wrapped in a black box, nestled in black tissue paper, tied with a blood red ribbon. It was like a Christmas present from a Goth friend, except even the Goths I knew didn't get so creepy as to gift blood-encrusted knives.

I actually hoped all the gunk on it was blood. There were some disturbing large chunks of something crusted onto the blade that I didn't even want to theorize about.

I knew better than to pick up a bloody knife. I wasn't like one of those idiots in TV and books who would carelessly leave their fingerprints all over potential murder weapons.

Also, when I hovered my hand over the knife, weird energy flowed through me, turning my stomach and chilling my blood. It was enough to make me snap the lid down, put the box in every plastic bag I had in my room, then wrap the whole thing in a blanket.

A blanket I'd have to burn later.

There was seriously bad juju coming from that box.

I'd just had a big snit about wanting to be alone, but this gift left on my doorstep was more important than my pride. So I gathered the bundle in my arms, ignored the nausea that swamped me, and trudged toward the professors' quarters.

I kicked Bane's door, hoping he wasn't still at Gareth's, and waited.

He flung the door open. His hair was damp and he'd slung a towel across his bare shoulders. Another towel was wrapped around his lean hips, and everything in between was gloriously bare.

"What are you doing here?" He leaned forward and peered down the hall.

"I got— Gah!" Bane's hand snapped out, grabbing me and virtually tossing me inside his room.

"You can't come to my rooms, Miss Jones." He slammed the door behind me. "What if someone had seen?"

I rolled my shoulder. "And you don't think someone seeing you dragging me into your room like a caveman would be more of a red flag? Jeez, you almost pulled my arm from its socket."

The hard lines in his face softened. "I apologize. Are you injured?"

"No. I'll be ok—"

"Then you need to leave." He held onto the ends of the towel around his neck and blew out a breath. "I mean it. You can't be seen here. It could destroy my career."

"Oh." I'd thought he'd been exaggerating the consequences of a professor-student relationship. Made it an excuse so he could hide from his feelings for me. I hadn't thought he could lose his job. I was an adult after all. Someone who could consent willingly.

My stomach sank. Or maybe it was still feeling sick from the bad juju box.

"Look, I'll leave, but I need to show you something." I set the box on a coffee table in the middle of his living room and tried to memorize everything in his room as

I unknotted the blanket. I probably wouldn't have a chance to be inside his apartment again.

There was more magic involved, of course, as his rooms stretched way past where his neighbors should be. His design style was sleek and modern. The sofa was black leather and chrome and looked uncomfortable as hell. One wall was brick, and the other was floor-to-ceiling windows with a view of… "Is that Paris?"

"The Eiffel Tower gave it away, didn't it?" he deadpanned.

I huffed. "No need to get snotty." I finally got the knot untied and started unwrapping the plastic bags. It took me longer than it should have as my eyes were more often on his chest than my fingers.

He watched as bag after bag drifted to his floor. "Is there anything in there or just an everlasting supply of shopping bags?"

Oh, he was in rare form tonight. Perhaps seeing me underneath Gareth had made something in him snap. A girl could dream, after all.

Finally, I pulled out the box. And then wiped my hands on my jeans. There was nothing unusual on the cardboard, but it felt foul against my skin just the same. "This was on my doorstep when I got home. And inside is a knife. One of those athame things I read about, I think. And..."

"And..." He flipped the lid off.

"And, it's not clean." Not physically, not magically. I didn't know how to describe it. Bane would just have to see for himself.

He frowned, pausing before he pulled the tissue paper back. His hand froze over the blade. "Oh, Goddess," he breathed.

Yeah, that wasn't a reassuring reaction.

"Do you recognize it?"

He swallowed. "I recognize the magic. It's been cursed."

"If I'd touched it...?" I pressed my hands to my stomach. I wasn't liking where this was going.

"Not cursed like that. You'd have been fine, if not a bit queasy." He strode to his desk and opened a drawer, pulling out a pocket knife. He flipped it open as he walked back. He nudged the athame with it. "Did you read the note?"

"There's a note?" I peered around his shoulder. A square of white paper was wedged under some of the tissue paper. If I'd picked the thing up, I would have seen it.

He carefully removed the small envelope.

"What kind of curse is it?" We hadn't cleared that one up yet. I didn't know if I wanted to move onto a note yet.

"A finder's curse." He sliced open the flap of the envelop. "It's placed on objects so they find their true owners." His dark brows knitted together.

"How is that a curse?"

He flipped the paper around, showing me what was written in a black scrawl.

*The chosen tool for the chosen one.*

My breaths were shallow. "And someone put that on my doorstep?"

"Or it found you on its own." He closed the box and picked it up. "I'm going to keep this in my safe. It shouldn't be left unprotected."

I followed him down a hall into a large bedroom. He flicked his fingers, and a painting of blue and gray swirls over his headboard slid sideways, revealing a very human looking safe.

"It didn't come to me." I crossed my arms over my chest, waiting until he turned before continuing. "Someone just thinks I'm this Chosen One and is messing with me. But it's not true, and we need to find the person the prophecy is really about."

His blue eyes were like icicles, stabbing into me with their intensity. "Need I remind you of the prophecy?"

He really didn't. I'd read that damn thing until my eyes bled. Heard it too many times in my dreams to ever forget a word.

But of course Bane would try to drive his point home.

"*She who is born to the witch who comes this year will be the alpha and the omega.*

*She will be the bringer of peace, and the advance guard of war.*

*Many magical creatures will die in the battle.*

*That which saves us will also destroy.*

*That which destroys, can also be destroyed.*

*She has the power to end our world.*

*Quidquid id est, timeo de ignotis.*"

"See?" I spread out my hands. "See how vague that is? How many witches were born the year my mother was? Thousands? Millions?" I kicked his mattress. "There has to be more to the prophecy for anyone to think it's about me." And the bringer of peace *and* war? This Druella who'd come up with the prophecy must have been off her rocker. It made no sense. And it was starting to piss me off how seriously everyone was taking it.

Bane slipped the towel from his neck and tossed it on his bed. Holding the knot of the one around his waist, he came to me. "You might be right. I hope you're right. But if you're not..." He looked past my shoulder, his jaw firming. "I have an idea. One that could protect everyone, including you."

"Great." I hoped his ideas were better than Dante's. Although, the information we'd taken from the council might still bear fruit. And if it did, I shouldn't hold octo-bastard against him. "Let's hear it."

He looked back at me. I couldn't quite read his expression. It almost looked like pity. "It could solve everything. But you aren't going to like it."

# Chapter Fourteen

"This is a bad idea." I sat cross-legged on the floor in Bane's living room. He'd moved the furniture out of the way and poured a protective circle of salt around me.

"You agreed to it," Bane reminded me. He'd changed into slacks and a cowl-necked sweater, taking away his lovely bare skin and the one reason I'd been happy to stay here. Drooling over Bane's chest and abs had acted like a tranquilizer. Now that it was gone, all my misgivings were clawing to come out.

"Yes, but stripping me of my magic seems a bit extreme." It had all sounded so reasonable when he'd laid out his plan. He'd cast a spell that would bind my powers. But, again, he'd been wearing nothing but a towel at the time. I could hardly be blamed for agreeing.

"We're not stripping your powers, merely blocking them for the time being." He lit a bundle of sage and waved the smoke toward the four corners of the room. "If your powers are blocked, then no one will be able to sense them. They'll think you nothing but a human, and a human wouldn't be the Chosen One. You can live a normal life until we figure this out."

I cocked my head. "And without my powers, there's less chance of me destroying the world, right?"

He paused, hand raised.

"Be honest. You think the prophecy is about me." I twisted my ring around my thumb. "What sort of odds are you giving me? Fifty-fifty that I'll be the savior or that I'll be the destroyer? Eighty-twenty?"

He placed the smoking sage into a copper bowl and rubbed his temple. "I do think the prophecy is about you. That spell I did earlier to find you—"

"The one that blew up the third floor?"

"It didn't blow—" He blew out a breath. "It was just the one room that was destroyed, but yes, that one. The spell was to locate the Chosen One. It was complicated. Dangerous. But's it is an accurate spell."

He gave me a sympathetic look that struck me straight down to my soul. "And it showed me you."

Complicated could mean he'd made a mistake. Bane was a good mage, maybe one of the best, but no one was one hundred percent accurate. Hope still lived.

I straightened out a smudge in the salt circle. "This... this is reversible, right?" I might not want to be the Chosen One, but I still wanted to be a witch. I couldn't imagine going back to my life as a regular human.

His eyes flickered. "Of course. If you want it to be."

"And what if I actually am supposed to save the world? How will I do that with no powers?"

He raised his eyebrow. "I hate to state the obvious, but your magical capabilities are spotty at best. I think the slew of powerful and competent witches who currently exist will be able to take up your slack."

I nodded. He was right. And this was for the best. I sucked in a deep breath as he began chanting. Of course, it was in Latin or some other ancient language so I couldn't understand shit. But maybe it was better that way.

My skin started to tingle.

I wouldn't know what had happened until it was done.

I ran my hand along my arm. It was burning now, the pain increasing with each word from his mouth. "Bane, wait."

He circled around me, his eyes remaining shut, his chanting only getting louder.

Something hooked under my rib cage, tearing at my insides, and I fell forward, my fingers digging into his rug.

This didn't feel right. *I* didn't feel right. I hadn't known about my magic for long, but it was a part of me now. And suddenly, I didn't want it taken from me. "Bane." I gasped. "Stop."

He either didn't hear me or ignored me. Circling and chanting. Endlessly circling.

I squeezed my eyes tight, trying to regain my balance. It felt like the ground was sliding out from under me.

Something deep inside my body howled. My hands clutched the floor, digging into the earth below. Which didn't make sense. We were on the fourth floor of the academy. I opened my eyes. My hands were still flat on the rug, my knuckles white.

Yet something inside clawed at the earth. Snarled. A caged beast.

Waiting to burst free.

"Sinjin!"

He paused and peered down at me.

The sage burned my eyes. I panted, my lungs never fully inflating.

He knelt in front of me. “I need to continue, do you understand? Any pain will be momentary.”

I snarled at him. Out and out snarled like a cornered animal.

Only, it wasn’t me. It used my mouth, glared through my eyes, But I didn’t control it.

Bane flinched. But he didn’t back away. “Delaney? You need to calm down.”

The beast within snarled again, and this time, I agreed with her. Who the hell has ever calmed down when someone tells them to calm down? No one, that’s who.

“Release...me...” The voice that came out of my mouth was deeper, rougher than usual. It was me, but not me, and I didn’t know how to wrap my mind around that.

“The spell isn’t done.” He held up a hand as though to touch me, then thought better of it. “I promise—”

I roared. My hand shot out, spraying salt over his slacks. I leapt, my palms smacking into his shoulders, knocking him onto his back.

I landed on top of him, my nails digging into his skin, my teeth bared. "You don't know enough to make promises," I hissed. "Do not try to defang me, warlock."

If I wasn't so bat-shit scared, I would have been kind of impressed with crazy me. But whereas before I'd felt like there was something inside me trying to get out, now I was the one trapped. I watched as my body moved without my control, listened as strange words fell from my mouth.

I was scared for Bane. Terrified for myself.

And weirdly turned on.

I inhaled, and every scent seemed sharper. I could smell the soap Bane had used. The mint of his mouthwash. And the little tinge of fear that oozed through his pores.

I straddled his lap, and even through his pants I could feel the tightness of his belly, the veins running the length of his cock.

I swiveled my hips. Whatever was inside me was apparently a little slut.

I couldn't complain, though. I felt the same tingle in my clit as she. Felt the slow slide of a bead of sweat wend its way down my spine.

I bent, inhaling the heat that rose from his throat. Then ran the tip of my tongue up to his jaw.

Delicious.

"Delaney," he said softly. "Where have you gone, Delaney?"

A sound emerged from my throat, somewhere between a chuckle and a growl. "Where I've always been. Within your reach, yet you never touch."

I wanted to nod. I agreed wholeheartedly with whoever was in control of my mouth at the moment. What the fuck was up with Bane anyway? I knew he wanted me. Could feel proof of it thickening against my slit. I could appreciate discipline, but it could be taken too far. Namely, when it got in the way of my fun times.

I threaded my fingers in his hair. It was soft as silk, and I twirled the ends around my fingers. "Don't you get tired of following the rules? I promise I won't tell if you give in just this once." I bent down, pressing my breasts to his chest. "Why won't you let yourself play?"

He gripped my hips. "This isn't you, Delaney. Come back to me."

I tugged his hair, yanking his head back. "Maybe you don't know me as well as you think." I nipped at his Adam's apple. Swirled my tongue in the hollow of his throat.

He grew harder beneath me, and I grinned. Everything he'd denied me would be mine tonight. Power surged through me, and I hummed against his skin. This was what being a witch felt like. Power. Control. Domination. The world was at my feet, mine to take.

Bane was mine to take.

I reached between us, flipped open the top button of his slacks. He grabbed my wrist when I started to ease down his zipper.

"No." His voice was harsh, his breathing heavy. "We can't do this."

I hissed. His pulse raced beneath my lips, and I bared my teeth and bit his throat until I tasted metal. Who was he to deny me?

I waited for him to strike. For the real battle to begin. My body jolted when he smoothed his palms up and down my back instead.

"It's okay, sweetheart," he murmured. "I've got you."

I released his throat, cocking my head. In point of fact, it seemed like I was the one who had him. Was the warlock stupid? Or playing a game?

But I couldn't deny his gentle massage eased my muscles. My body curled around his. If I'd been a cat, I would have purred.

"You don't have to worry," he said. "No more spells for tonight. Delaney can come back. She's safe now."

Safe? I didn't know if that was possible. Not anymore.

My body shook, and Bane held my tighter. He murmured soft words in my ear. The heat from his hands sent calming waves pulsing into my flesh.

The backs of my eyes burned, and I knew I was back. The bitchy witch wouldn't want to cry at this moment. She'd be either dry humping the hottie between her thighs or tearing his throat out.

"Bane?" I whispered.

"Yes, sweetheart?"

"I think I'm in trouble." And I let the tears fall onto his neck.

# Chapter Fifteen

I hadn't slept last night. I'd wanted to ask Bane if I could spend the night with him. No screwing around, just him and his magic hands holding me close. But I'd been too chicken, not wanting him to see my weakness.

I mean, if he'd instigated some screwing around, I probably would have been okay with it. It could have helped me take my mind off of how fucked I was.

For the first time since all this magic stuff had gone down, I thought I might actually be the Chosen One.

And if the violent bitch inside of me was any indication, the odds were leaning more eighty-twenty that I would be the destroyer of the world. I hadn't felt much like saving anything last night. I'd wanted to possess. Dominate. And those weren't happy, healthy feelings. If I were in an RPG, I'd be leaning more chaotic evil, no doubt.

I dragged through the breakfast line. When I bypassed the peanut butter waffles for a steaming cup of coffee, I knew I must really be depressed.

Someone jostled my arm. There was a screech. A crash of dishes. I turned.

Ophelia stood feet from me, fists clenched, body shaking. And thick globules of grits oozed down her fuchsia colored top.

Hazel jostled my elbow again. "Sorry about that," she said with a smile as fake as a Kardashian's ass. "The tray just slipped." She raised her hands in an 'oopsie' gesture, grabbed my arm, and pulled me to a table in the corner where Quincy sat with a tower of books to his left.

"What was that about?" I took a sip of coffee and grimaced. I'd been dragged away before I could add my customary pint of sugar.

"That was me saving your C and D grade." Hazel reached over to Quincy's tray and snagged a banana. "She was about to spell your ass."

"Oh." It kind of would have been nice to have that over with. No more looking over my shoulder. No more high noon standoffs whenever we came across each other. I was tired of having things hanging over my head.

"'Oh'?" Hazel narrowed her eyes. "What's with you?"

I shrugged, taking another sip of my bitter-ass coffee. It seemed like a metaphor for my life. "Ophelia can win this one. I don't care."

Hazel and Quincy shot each other looks I didn't appreciate. Twin ones of surprise and disappointment.

Hazel leaned over the table and planted her finger on it. "Get it together, girl. You almost failed the final." She shook her head, setting her black page boy to swinging. "And don't ever give any win to Ophelia. That witch is a bitch."

My lips twitched. "Tell me how you really feel?"

She grabbed an apple from Quincy's tray and threw it at me.

I snatched it from the air. Jeez, how much fruit did that boy eat? Did he have some sort of intestinal problem?

"All I'm saying is I don't like this new, defeatist Delaney." Hazel crossed her arms. "We want our fighter back."

Quincy nodded stoutly.

They were right. One bad night shouldn't be enough to knock me down. I stretched, trying to get some blood flow to energize my body. "Okay. I'll sulk when I'm dead. Delaney Giantslayer Jones is back in action."

Something knocked into the back of my head. A blueberry muffin bounced off the floor, a large wedge breaking off.

I swung around. The triplets smirked from the table next to us. One had his arm tossed over the back of Ophelia's chair. "Giantslayer?" one of the brothers asked. I didn't know which Bastardo he was, and I didn't care. "I like Hotpants Jones much better. At least when you wore those pink spandex shorts in the ring you gave the audience something to enjoy. You're fighting skills sure didn't."

My face burned, and I wished I could dredge up my evil bitch from last night to wipe that smug smile off his face. Worse, I kind of wanted to pick up that moist, delicious looking muffin and eat the rest of it. I was officially having a sad morning.

I raised my chin. "Either name you choose, I can kick your ass. Anything else you want to say?"

Hazel snickered. "Want any eggs with those grits, Ophelia? I can make sure your shirt gets a complete meal."

Ophelia cracked the knuckles of her right hand, her eyes spitting fire.

"Our father will be so disappointed when he hears of the caliber of student the Raven Academy has started to accept." One of the other creepy triplets flicked his long, dishwater-blond hair behind his shoulder. "I think this school is in need of a cleansing."

"Judging by the way you sit like you have a stick in your ass, I bet you're used to a good cleanse," I said. I stood and grabbed half of Quincy's books. "Much as I'd love to continue this, I have work to do." I had no work to do, but I didn't have the energy to spar. And this was feeling way too much like high school for my liking.

Hazel and Quincy followed me up. We stalked past their table, me deftly avoiding the long leg one of the blond Bastardos stuck out. Quincy wasn't so lucky. He stumbled but didn't fall, and I counted that as a victory.

And I snagged a muffin on my way out. A victory for my stomach.

"Do you actually have work?" Hazel asked.

"Of course not." I took a huge bite of the muffin and checked the time. Still a half hour until Cryptozoology.

"You might now." Hazel slid a book out from the stack I held and placed it on top. "Quincy found something in here. Something we might be able to use."

I read the title. "*Reflections on Magic, Mysticism, and Mayhem*. Sounds like a real page-turner."

"It's an autobiography by Druella Bancroft." Hazel led us down the hall and to a stone window seat. The big bay windows looked out upon a massive magnolia tree.

Hazel settled onto one of the pillows. "Druella had a sister, Hedwig Bancroft, one who Druella said was a better seer than her. She actually sounded kind of jealous and bitchy about it." Hazel twisted her lips. "Power breeds competition, I guess."

"And this helps me how?" I eyed the thick tome and sank down next to her. I needed to read as much about the woman who'd marked me as a target as I could, but the size of that thing was intimidating.

"Hedwig is still alive. She lives in some little village in Wales."

I gave her the keep-going motion. "Still not seeing how this helps."

Hazel huffed out a breath, her bangs floating up before resettling around her narrow face. "You're an only child so maybe you don't get this, but sisters tell each other things. They talk. And if one sister prophesied the end of the world, I'd think she'd have a big ass confab about it with her only sister. Tell her details that might not be in the official prophecy."

I tucked my leg under me, my heart kicking into higher gear. "Do you really think she could tell us something more? Something useful?" Like maybe Druella had said the Chosen One would be a six-foot Amazonian, thereby knocking me out of contention.

Hazel covered my hand with her own and squeezed. "I don't know for certain, but it's worth a shot. When it comes to something like the end of the world, we should leave no avenue unexplored."

My chest warmed. Such a small thing, Hazel's hand on mine. Her support. But it meant the world. I didn't feel alone or afraid anymore. Well, maybe a little afraid still. After all, I'd lost control last night when Bane had threatened my magical side. That didn't make me feel safe or secure.

But not alone? Yeah, that one, a hundred percent.

"Can we call her?" Maybe Facetime would be best. It's harder to say no to someone if you're looking her in the eyes.

Quincy shifted, adjusting his hold on his books.

Hazel flicked a glance at him. "Yeah, she's a bit of a hermit. We tried looking her number up, but she's completely unlisted. We only found her address through property tax records. Other than that, she has no internet profile."

That was... weird. But then, so was my life. Me and Hedwig might get on like a house on fire. A saying I never understood but I didn't have time to worry about that now. "So what are you suggesting?"

"That we go visit her. In person. Face to face. It will be much harder to evade our questions."

Which mirrored my thoughts about Facetime, but knocking on someone's door just seemed pushy. "I don't know...."

Hazel pinched her lips together. "You're still thinking like a normal witch. Not one who is facing an apocalypse. We don't have time to be timid. Or *polite*." She said polite like it was a dirty word, and I couldn't help but smile.

"Okay, you're right." The men in my life wouldn't be happy with this latest excursion. They liked me locked down at the academy where I was safe. I chewed my lip and stared outside, trying to figure out the best way to tell them.

After I returned from Wales was probably best.

The swaying branches of the magnolia tree outside the window seemed to agree. It was like they were waving us off on our journey.

"I guess we're going to Wales," I said.

Hazel clapped. "Sweet. Field trip."

"Move!" Quincy's voice boomed around us, the urgency in the one word brooking no questions. Hazel and I threw ourselves to the floor, books flying, a shiver of dread working its way down my spine a moment before the world exploded.

# Chapter Sixteen

Shards of glass and bits of crumbled stone scratched my body moments before something hard and heavy landed on top of me.

I groaned. I had no idea what had just happened, but if I'd died, the afterlife was crappy. The pressure on my back was immense. Something sharp was poking way too close to my asshole for comfort. And... I sniffed. Well, at least it smelled heavenly.

"Get it off them!"

There were more shouts. The sounds of shoes crunching over glass and strained grunting. Finally, finally, the pressure eased off my back. I paid the sound of ripping denim no mind, not caring if my jeans were torn to shreds. I could fill my lungs again, and that was the sweetest feeling there was.

Memories of Gareth's and Dante's hands on my body filled my head.

Well, breathing was one of the top three awesome feelings at least.

Quincy pushed my shoulder, as if checking I was alive, and I rolled to my side and held up a hand. "I'm fine. Hazel?"

"Here." She sat against the wall, scowling down at her legs. "And I want a refund. These tights were supposed to be run proof. The Facebook ad showed some chick running a cheese grater over them without tearing." She plucked at the black nylon, pulling at the two gashes that exposed her skin beneath.

And the deep scratches that oozed blood.

"Who the hell cares about your tights?" I pushed up on one arm, and fell back down to my butt. I waved off Quincy's hand. "You need to see a doctor. Or at least a big-ass box of band-aids."

I pushed up again and managed to get to my feet. My legs wobbled, pain arcing from the base of my spine down my legs. Maybe I was the one who needed a doctor.

"I'm fine." Hazel held out her hands and Quincy hurried to her, pulling her to her feet. "This tights company won't be after I leave them a scathing review."

I dropped my chin to my chest and felt my shoulders relax. She was all right. I didn't like seeing blood on my friend, but if she could joke about her tights, she had to be okay.

She pulled her phone from her pocket and started typing away, eyes narrowed.

Okay, so maybe she hadn't been joking.

I stepped away from the magnolia tree that had taken a header into the academy. The top branch was bare and spiky, the perfect shape to impale unsuspecting window-sitters.

"Was there a tornado or something?" I looked out the gaping hole in the stone wall at clear blue skies.

Quincy shook his head.

"Could have been a microburst," Hazel said, her face still buried in her phone.

"I've never seen anything like it." One of the students who'd helped pull it off us shook his head. "It came through the window like a rocket."

I thanked everyone still milling around. A flash of dirty-blond hair on the end of the hall drew my gaze. One of the fucklets, and yes, that was my new name for the triplets, leaned against the wall, arms crossed over his chest.

He gave me a slow nod. A congratulations on still being alive? Judgment that I didn't duck faster? Regardless, I noticed he hadn't been one of the students to come rushing to help.

As my adrenalin eased, my body cooled. I ran my hands up and down my arms. Had this been an accident? Trees did fall. But the angle of it, the way the tree had speared into the window I was seated at, seemed intentional.

Bane and the headmistress rushed around the corner. When Bane saw me, his shoulders dropped away from his ears. The tension in his face relaxed, and he drank me up in his gaze.

More importantly, there was no lingering fear or weirdness from last night. He'd assured me before I'd left his room that we were fine. That he didn't see me as the crazed bitch who had drawn blood. But I hadn't believed him until now.

When Headmistress Dreadmoon saw me, her face scrunched in annoyance.

I preferred Bane's expression.

"Miss Jones, what has happened here?" Dreadmoon panted to a stop next to me, her long tie-dyed skirt swirling. She flailed her hands at the magnolia tree. "What is the meaning of this?"

"A weak root system?" I guessed. Wouldn't that explanation be nice?

She exhaled noisily. "Our trees don't have weak roots. Professor Clovern tends to every plant on academy property."

"And he's been gone for several weeks now." Bane's eyes narrowed as he checked me over. He slipped from his jacket. He wore a navy turtleneck, probably to hide my bite mark, the color of it bringing out the blue of his eyes.

I'd never known a man could look so good in a turtleneck.

"Perhaps any spells he's put on the plants have weakened," he said. "We should ask Killough to monitor the flora as the new professor of Herbology." Stepping to my side, he settled his tweed jacket over my shoulders. He tugged at the back hem, his hand grazing against the skin on my upper thigh.

The bare skin.

I clutched my torn jeans, feeling the edges of the triangle that had been ripped from the bottom.

"The jacket should cover it. No need to expose yourself to anyone else." His gaze heated. He bit his lower lip, and when he tugged again at the back hem, his hand lingered a little longer than necessary against my skin.

And I wasn't complaining.

Then, like a rubber band, his expression snapped back to normal. Bored. Disdainful. He stepped back, and even with his coat I felt cold again.

"I fail to understand how these accidents keep happening to you." Dreadmoon pulled a tablet out from her billowing vest. "Now I need to call a stone mason, a glazier, and someone to chop up and remove the tree."

"She hardly asked for the tree to almost kill her, Headmistress." Bane stepped to the edge of the rubble and peered outside. "You can't lay the blame for this one at her feet."

I snuggled deeper into his jacket. He might wear a mask of indifference, but I knew better. I drew my fingers over the soft suede on the sleeves.

I was wearing Bane's jacket, the sexy one with the elbow patches. I lifted up the flap of the collar and buried my nose in it. It smelled like licorice, cherry wood, and man. Like Bane. There wasn't a chance in hell he was getting this back.

"I'll escort the students to the infirmary." Bane spread his arms, gesturing for us to gather to him. He herded Hazel, Quincy, and I down the hall, leaving the headmistress glaring at her to-do list on her tablet.

"We don't need to see the healers," Hazel said.

"Those are some nasty looking cuts on your legs, Miss Willowtree." Bane placed his hand on my lower back and guided me up the first couple steps toward the medical ward. I didn't mind near-death experiences so much if it meant Bane eased his no-touching rules. "We wouldn't want them to become infected."

"No, I guess *we* wouldn't." Hazel didn't sound nearly so taken with Bane's mannerisms.

I shrugged mentally. To each her own. All I knew was Bane's assertive attitude did it for me. All of the men in my life did it for me, and all for different reasons.

Dante was my comfort, like a warm blanket. A sexy, warm blanket who would always be there to provide unfailing support and love.

Gareth unlocked something wild in me. Let me act out my darkest fantasies without fear of hurting him. He called to the primal part of my soul. I didn't have to wonder how it would be to sleep with him. I already knew. Hot. Wild. Rough.

And Bane... Bane challenged me. Made me want to strive to be my best. And a small part of myself, one I'd never admit to Hazel or anyone, loved his domineering ways. Craved his guidance and discipline. I wanted to bend over his desk. Have him pin my hands behind my back as he took me deep.

My core clenched. Sweat beaded on my lower back, but I didn't take off Bane's coat. I pulled the front of my shirt away from my chest and flapped it, trying to bring in some airflow.

Bane opened the door to the infirmary and waved Hazel inside. Quincy padded after her.

I took a step forward, but Bane put his hand on my shoulder, stopping me. "A moment, Miss Jones."

The door eased shut. Bane waited for the click of the latch before speaking. "Was this an attack?"

"I don't know." I leaned back against the wall. "But Dreadmoon is probably right. With me, it seems likely. I'd hoped that after Thanness died, I'd have had some peace and quiet in the academy for a while."

Except Thanness hadn't just died. I'd killed him. Sort of. I swallowed, the back of my throat burning.

I still didn't like to think of that night. I hadn't talked about it with anyone. They'd assumed whatever they'd assumed, and we'd let it lie at that.

Bane crossed his arms over his chest. "I don't like it."

Yeah, I wasn't too thrilled about almost being a shish kebob, either. "Look, Quincy and Hazel found something. Druella Bancroft had a sister. Hedwig. She's still alive and living in Wales—"

"No."

"—and we thought…." I trailed off. "No? What do you mean no?"

"No, I don't have time to take you to Wales to talk to Druella's sister. I have too much to do, especially after this latest incident." A door opened down the hall, and a professor exited. Bane shifted, putting his body between me and the man's curious gaze.

We waited until the man's footsteps had faded. "You don't have to come with us," I said. "We could—"

"Definitely not." He exhaled heavily. "With all that's happening, now is not the time to act recklessly. You need to be smart. And safe."

"Yeah, because it's so safe here," I snarked.

That muscle in his jaw ticked. The one that made me want to rock up onto my toes and lick it. The one that made me want to push him farther, see if I could get him to snap.

He didn't snap. He said in an excessively cool voice, "Regardless, my answer is still no. You will stay here, and I'll make certain it's safe for you. Now, go let the healer take a look at you. Don't think I didn't notice you walking stiffly." And with one last muscle twitch, he turned on his heel and stalked away.

"Better to walk stiff than act stiff," I shouted after his retreating back. Not the cleverest of come-backs, but it did make his stride hitch and his shoulders tense before turning the corner.

I slumped against the wall. He was such a condescending prick. It was probably a good thing he'd never let us cross a line. I wouldn't want someone so infuriating in my bed. Good riddance.

If only I could convince myself of that.

The door hissed open beside me and Hazel popped her head out. "The healer can see you now."

I flapped my hand. "I'm fine." Except for a bad case of wanting what I couldn't have. "I'll meet you and Quincy at the portal at midnight. We go to Hedwig's tonight."

# Chapter Seventeen

The cottage was half-buried in a rolling hillside, its thatched-roof fusing into the grass seamlessly. A cheery stream of smoke floated up from one of the six narrow chimneys. I know Bane said magic didn't have anything to do with Harry Potter, but this witch's cottage in Wales was something I'd only have believed existed in the movies. If not Harry Potter, then Lord of the Rings in that hobbit village.

It was adorable.

I eyed the smoke again. And a bit of a fire hazard. Should you burn wood when your roof was made of straw?

Hazel knocked as I continued to squint at the roof. "What does 'get on like a house on fire' even mean?" I asked. Because it was stupid and irrelevant, that question had been gnawing at me like a stray on a day-old bone. "I mean, I know it means two people get along well, but what does that have to do with a house burning?"

The squat front door swung open to complete blackness. A deep voice made the hinges on the door shake. "If you burn my house down, I will curse you. Turn you into a kangaroo with a three-foot dick. Every time you hop, you'll bang that dick on the ground. Thump, thump, thump goes the dick. It will be ex-cru-ciating."

Hazel and Quincy glanced at each other, then each took a large step to the side. Leaving me alone in the doorway facing a scarily dick-happy witch.

Traitors. Smart traitors, but traitors nonetheless.

"Uh, I'm not planning on burning your house down." I cleared my throat and tried to make my voice sound friendly and reassuring. As opposite from an arsonist or door-to-door salesman as I could.

As curses went, turning into a kangaroo with a three-foot dick sounded amazingly horrible. And something I wanted to avoid at all costs. "I was just asking what the saying 'get on like a house on fire' means."

"Oh." The blackness shifted. "Stupid saying. Now go away."

The door began to swing shut, and I jammed my foot in the opening. "Wait!" I grimaced at the pinch to my toes. "We came a long way to talk to you. It's really important."

A form emerged from the darkness. Hunched. Wrinkled. But with the most razor-sharp gaze I'd ever seen in a pair of eyes.

That gaze examined me from foot to head. The wizened old woman pursed her lips.

"I didn't recognize you with that crazy hair." The witch tilted her head. "I'd wondered if you'd come."

"You know me?"

Her huff turned into a coughing attack, and I looked uneasily at Hazel and Quincy. Normally I'd pound someone on the back if they were coughing like that, but that didn't seem safe with this woman. She seemed so frail I'd probably knock her into next week.

Hazel shrugged.

Quincy reached into his trouser pocket and pulled out a foil-wrapped lozenge. "Cough drop?"

I took it from him and handed it to the woman. She swiped it from my hand, unwrapped it, and popped it in her mouth. "Damn cauldrons," she rasped when she was finally able to talk. "Smoke's not good for your lungs."

"I can see that." I shifted my weight. "You are Hedwig Bancroft, right? Druella's sister?"

"Dru was *my* sister." The wrinkles on her eyes grew even more wrinkly with her squint.

I didn't get the distinction. "Oka-aay. We were hoping—"

"I know what you want." She threw the wrapper over her shoulder. "Come on, you three. Let's talk inside."

I bent to go through the doorway and entered into a cluttered sitting room. Boxes and crates were stacked haphazardly around the room, tilting precariously. Brightly colored scarves were draped over every surface. It seemed Hedwig was a bit of a hoarder, and I wondered how she could live in here.

My gaze followed her curled back as she waddled toward a side door. Her spine looked like a candy cane.

I straightened and threw my shoulders back. Posture was important. And milk. I needed to start drinking more milk.

My friends followed me into the next room. I blinked when Hedwig flipped on the lights.

And blinked again when my eyes finally focused on what appeared before me.

My lungs froze. I stumbled in a circle, taking in the paintings that covered every inch of wall space in the room.

Every painting was of a woman.

Every painting was of me.

"Holy shit." Hazel twisted. "They're you. They're all you."

They all showed me with my natural brown hair. I tossed the end of my blue ponytail over my shoulder. Whoever had painted these hadn't known of my killer style. But it was my nose. My eyes and lips. They weren't photograph quality paintings, but the images were undeniably all of me.

Hazel faced me, her eyes wide. "You really are the Chosen One."

Hedwig snorted. "Chosen One. What a bunch of malarkey."

"Wait." My heart leapt in hope. "I'm not the one named in your sister's prophecy?"

Hedwig looked heavenward. "Look around you. My sister was obsessed. Of course, you're the one in the prophecy. She saw you in her dreams." She sniffed. "I didn't think you'd be so stupid."

I bit my tongue. It wouldn't be cool to cuss out an old woman. "Then what did you mean by malarkey?"

"A prophecy doesn't determine your life." Faster than an old woman had any right to move, Hedwig shot her hand out, gripping my biceps. "You make your own destiny. There is nothing chosen, or predetermined, about anyone."

"But Ba— a warlock I know said a prophecy made by a good witch is accurate like 99.9 percent of the time." And Bane seemed to be right about that same amount. Except when it came to the important things, like a relationship between us. His reluctance there felt dead wrong to me.

"That's true. And my sister was good," Hedwig admitted. "But prophecies have a tendency to be self-fulfilling." She pointed a gnarled finger at me. "You were named in a prophecy about battling for the fate of the world. Now you're drawn into the war. If you hadn't been in the prophecy, would you be involved? Or would you be living your life in Hoboken, never the wiser."

"Detroit." But I took her meaning. If no one was trying to kill me, would I be so gung-ho about joining in this fight? I'd like to think that I'd do the right thing, but I also didn't want to die for the cause.

Hedwig turned and toddled toward the door. "Near the end of her life, Druella agreed with me. That's why she didn't tell anyone about her second prophecy." And after landing that bombshell, she disappeared into her living room.

I looked at Hazel. She blinked, then turned owl eyes on Quincy.

"Holy fuck," he said.

My thoughts exactly.

I tore after the old witch. "Wait. What second prophecy?"

She kept walking.

"What second prophecy?" I darted in front of her before she could make the kitchen, blocking her way with my body. My chest heaved. I was in enough trouble with one damn prophecy. What supreme being hated me enough to burden me with two?

Hedwig frowned. "My eggs should be done, girl. Out of my way."

"Not until you tell me the second prophecy." I crossed my arms over my chest. Over-cooked eggs be damned. She wasn't leaving until I got my answers.

A low rumble emerged from her chest, but I stood firm.

"Fine," she huffed. "It went something like, 'With the power of four, there will be magic enough to end the war. With the power of four, the world will be changed forevermore.'"

"Something like that? Or exactly like that?" My stomach twisted. More cryptic BS. Why couldn't a friggin' prophecy come with dates and times? First and last names?

"Exactly that." Hedwig glared. "Can I eat my breakfast now?"

I stepped aside. "Thank you. If you think of anything else...."

The witch snorted. "All I can think about is my empty stomach." She pushed past me. "You can show yourselves—"

She froze, her body going stiff.

"Miss Bancroft?" I gripped her shoulder. "Hedwig?"

Her hand shot out, her fingers digging into my arm like claws. Her eyes stared forward, unseeing. Or seeing something that no one else did.

"*Beware, child.*" Her voice was a creepy intonation. It sounded like Hedwig, only not.

I darted a glance at Hazel but she only shrugged. No help there.

"*Darkness surrounds you. Is closer than you think. The newcomer isn't your friend. The school is in his control.*"

I peeled her nails from my flesh, wincing. I didn't see how the darkness could be any closer. I'd almost been stabbed by a tree yesterday. That seemed pretty damn close.

But who was the newcomer to the academy? The fucklets were new, but there were three of them, and Hedwig seemed to be talking about one person. The tall, pale, and beautiful vampire flashed into my mind. Professor Killough was the newest professor to Raven. And I didn't quite trust his friendliness. Perhaps it was time to give him a closer look.

Or perhaps Hedwig was just batshit crazy.

"I'm not nuts." She shook her head, her eyes clearing. "I don't have prophecies like my sister, but my visions of the immediate future are never wrong. Well, hardly ever."

"Druella's autobiography talked about how powerful her sister was," Hazel reminded me. "But what does it mean? Who controls the school, and how?"

That was a common theme when it came to these damn visions. I was getting tired of all of them. "I guess we'll find out." I nodded to Hedwig. She seemed nice enough, but suddenly I wanted far away from her. From this whole business. I stalked to the front door, my friends trailing behind.

"Remember," Hedwig said when my hand was on the knob. "You choose your own destiny. You choose whether to be the savior or the destroyer."

"Why would I choose to destroy? If I get a choice, then I choose saving the world."

She barked out a laugh. "You can't think of anything that would make you turn your back on your values? There's no temptation great enough to make you betray your ideals?"

My shoulders tensed. "Nothing I want enough where I'd agree to destroy the entire world." Of that I was certain.

"Druella didn't foretell the end of the whole world. Just the end of the magical world. The war is between our kind." Hedwig sniffed. "Humans will be okay except for some collateral damage."

That... was actually reassuring. I mean, the magical world ending was horrifying, but it wasn't the total annihilation I'd thought the prophecy meant. But I didn't think Hazel and Quincy or any of the men in my life would find the same solace in that.

"That's just as bad," Hazel said, proving me right.

"But if she's right that we get to choose our destinies, then we don't have anything to worry about." I tucked my arm through Hazel's and pulled her outside, into the warm sunlight. I breathed in the scents of cut grass and honeysuckle, this very British morning seeming much cheerier than when we went into the cottage.

I wanted to believe Hedwig, that I was in control of my own future. It was how I'd always lived my life. The one thing my father had taught me was that I was responsible for my own actions. It had made my decision to leave his house that much easier. Had made me stay in the gym longer than any of the other fighters, knowing my dedication would eventually pay off. There was a power in taking responsibility for your life. If nothing else came from this trip to Wales, the reminder that I controlled my own life made it worthwhile.

Quincy stopped next to us, tipping his face back and breathing deeply.

"It *is* nice to get away from the academy once in a while," Hazel said.

"Ain't that the truth." The winding dirt road curved around a hill. Some sort of blue bird was chirping his ass off. I wanted to spend more time here, away from the stresses of the academy. But it wasn't possible. "I just have one question."

"What's that?" Hazel bent and plucked a yellow bud from a nearby bush.

"How do we get back?" The permanent portal hidden in Raven took us where we directed, but there was no corresponding portal here. And neither my friends nor I knew how to create one.

Hazel blew out her cheeks, the air inside releasing with a pop. "Huh."

"Yeah. Huh." In our eagerness to talk to Hedwig, we really hadn't planned this all the way through. I pulled my phone from my back pocket, took a panoramic picture of our surroundings, and sent it to Bane. He needed to know exactly what the space looked like in order to create a portal.

Then I made a call I really didn't want to. When Bane picked up, I said, "Hey. Don't be mad, but we need a lift."

# Chapter Eighteen

Bane was mad. A pacing-his-office, running-his-hands-through-his-hair kind of mad.

It was hot.

"What were you thinking, Miss Jones?" He fisted his hands on his lean hips. "After I specifically told you—"

"Yeah, that was your first mistake." I crossed one leg over the other and let my foot swing. "When someone tells me to do something I generally do the opposite. You really should know this about me by now." I smoothed my palms over the arm of my chair. The leather guest chairs in his office were soft and comfy. And just the right height to lean forward, unzip Bane's—

"Reckless. Irresponsible. And did you even think of your friends?" He stalked behind his desk and placed his palms on the dark wood. "You have a target on your back, and by inviting them with you outside these walls, you put them in danger, too."

I tried to look contrite. It wasn't really a look I was familiar with, and I could tell by Bane's expression that I hadn't pulled it off. "Look, we all got back okay, and besides, it was worth it. Hedwig said the prophecy doesn't mean all that much. That I'm in control of my own destiny. That was worth the trip right there."

His eyebrows drew down. His lips thinned. And that muscle in his jaw went tick, tick, tick.

I thought he might be having a heart attack. Or that he was about to spell me into submission. I raised my hands. "You have to chill out. Nothing went wrong. We're all fine. I'm fine."

He inhaled sharply, his laser-sharp gaze boring a hole into me.

I shifted on my seat. The intensity in his eyes was doing funny things to me. Every naughty teacher-student fantasy I'd ever had came roaring back to life. "Uh, you're not going to get out a ruler. Are you?" I asked, hopefulness tinging my words.

He blew out an exasperated sigh. "Christ. I'm not going to rap your knuckles, Delaney." He dropped into his chair and laced his fingers together behind his neck. His starched white shirt stretched across a strong chest and flat stomach.

I bit my lip. If I told him I'd thought of him smacking another part of my anatomy, would that piss him off more? Or turn him on?

"I don't know what goes through your mind sometimes." He shook his head, disappointment written across his features. "You're as impulsive as a child."

I was going with pissing him off more. Sexy times seemed a distant possibility with his attitude.

Which was fine, because he was starting to annoy me now, too. "I'm not a child. And I refuse to be treated like a prisoner. Now, do you want to continue to act like a condescending prick, or would you like to hear about Druella's second prophecy?"

He stopped breathing. His body froze into stone. "A second prophecy?"

I read it to him, thankful that Hazel had thought to type it into my phone while we'd waited for Bane in Wales.

"And her sister told you this came from Druella?"

I nodded. "But did you miss the part where she also said prophecies were malarkey? We all create our own destiny."

Bane closed his eyes and held out his hands. A thick book popped into them, dust drifting from the worn, brown cover. "It's your destiny. Got it. Check." He flipped open the book, running through the pages like he was searching for a specific chapter.

"That's not..." My shoulders sagged. Why bother? He was convinced of my role in the war between magical beings, and at this point, what did it matter? Because of the prophecy, I was involved now. I would be a part of it. It was useless to keep arguing the point.

I chewed on the inside of my cheek. "Uh, there was something else about Hedwig." I really didn't want to tell him about the warning she'd delivered. It might make him decide to put me under lock and key. But it was probably too important to keep to myself.

"Is she still a hoarder?" he asked absently, He ran his finger down a page. "I've told her we're going to find her buried under her boxes one day."

"No, um, well yes, but that's not—"

"I have a lot of research to do, Miss Jones." He flipped to another page. "Can you please stop stammering and get to the point?"

My skin flushed hot. I gripped the armrest of my chair. “No point,” I said. “Just making conversation, but I’ll leave you to it.” I knew it was stupid to let my anger make my decision, but like hell I was going to tell him anything more when he was acting like this. And besides, it’s not like the warning helped us in any way. We already knew people were trying to kill me, and Hedwig’s vision was very nonspecific. This was something I’d keep between me and Hazel and Quincy.

He pulled a pad of paper toward him and took some notes. “If you could see fit to stay within academy walls for the foreseeable future, I’d be most appreciative.”

“Sure.” Unless another lead arose that my friends and I could check out.

Because one thing was damn certain.

I pushed to my feet and started for his door.

I was done being a passive observer to my destiny, whatever it would be.

I was back to being a woman of action.

# Chapter Nineteen

"Do you see her? Is she still there?"

Hazel ducked her head around the corner of the wall and jerked it back as quickly. "Yes, just like the past one hundred times you've asked. Although no one can read forever. Even as slow as Ophelia is, she's got to finish that book eventually. Get on with it."

I shook out my hands, trying to ease the nervous energy flowing through me. It was worse than when I went in the ring with Monster Mike, and I'd known that would be quick and ugly from the get-go.

But spelling someone was different than swinging a fist. I had control over my punches. Knew just the right amount of force to put behind them. Magic was still an iffy proposition for me. I didn't like Ophelia, and this was a part of my C and D final, but I didn't want to actually do any damage.

I bobbed on my toes, trying to get in the right headset. "Step out. Let her see me. Then hit her with my itching spell." I could do that. And I liked the spell I'd come up with. One minute of it feeling like ants were skittering all over your body, and then it was done.

Neat. Clean. Simple. And a definite passing grade.

I sidled past Hazel, who'd insisted on watching me spell Ophelia, and gave my own peek around the corner.

Ophelia sat on a wide burgundy chair, her ostrich leather bag tucked by her side, her head on her fist as she yawned.

I guessed whatever she was reading wasn't the latest thriller. But she looked completely unaware of her surroundings. Defenseless. The perfect time to spell her.

I pulled back and leaned against the library wall. I focused on my breathing until I got a little light-headed.

Hazel smacked my shoulder. "Stop procrastinating and just do it."

"What if something goes wrong?" I asked. "What if it doesn't wear off in a minute." Ophelia was a PITA, but she didn't deserve to scratch her skin raw because of my magic.

"Then she goes to the healers and gets the spell reversed." Hazel sighed. "Don't worry so much. And this is a class assignment. You have to do it."

"Right." And I would. Just as soon as I felt the moment was perfectly right. I peered around the edge again. Ophelia had put the book down on her lap. And she looked straight at me.

"Shit. She saw me." I stepped fully into her line of vision. No more time to waste. I gathered my intention into my core, felt the small buzz that came with the gathering of my magic.

"Do it, do it, do it," Hazel chanted behind me. Ruining my concentration, I might add.

"I don't know if I can. I'm not angry right now." I felt guilty instead, and that didn't seem to be an emotion that gave me power.

"How can you not be mad?" Hazel asked. "She's horrible, and has done horrible things. To you, to all of us." She poked my back. "Now make her pay."

I nodded. Put up my hands. Felt my magic stream through my body.

And paused. "Wait. She's... smiling at me?" That didn't make sense. My hands lowered an inch. Should I smile back? Maybe give her a friendly wave? She had to know I was about to spell her. Why wasn't she fighting back?

Hazel stepped to my side. "She's not just smiling. That bitch is laughing at you."

I narrowed my eyes. Hazel was right. Ophelia's smile had turned from a full-blown smirk to a head-thrown-back, you're-so-pathetic kind of laugh.

A rush of heat flushed through my body. She thought I was too pitiful to even defend against. Too powerless to hurt her.

My palms tingled. The bitch was going down.

My intention was gone. All I felt was power. Power gathering at my core, shooting through my body, down my arms, and out of my hands.

The air shimmered a dusty silver as my spell flew through it.

And Ophelia didn't even bother to stop laughing.

Not until the spell veered off target and hit her prized purse. Making it explode into flakes of ostrich skin and puffs of stuffing.

Ophelia shrieked, her book flying, her eyes wide in terror. When she saw what was left of her bag, smoldering on the chair beside her, those eyes went squinty and dark, and Hazel and I took a hasty step back.

"I've got to go, Daddy," Ophelia yelled. She flicked her wrist just as Hazel and I ducked behind the wall.

"I think she was talking to her dad on that Pic Portal." Hazel sidled down the hall. "That might have been an illegal attack since she didn't see you standing there."

"Ya think?" I trotted past Hazel. There was a time for stealth, and there was a time to get the fuck outta Dodge. This was the latter. Ophelia could be scary on a good day. I'd just destroyed her prized gift from her father. "Tell no one about this," I hissed to Hazel. "No one."

She nodded as she raced past me. Neither of us wanted to be the one Ophelia found when she started looking. But I had longer legs than my friend, and I overtook her as we hit the great hall.

"Wait." She bent at the waist, sucking down air. "Act cool."

I nodded. Cool. I could do that. I leaned against the wall and checked my nails, because that was something girls totally did. "So, since that went so well, want to help me find Professor Killough? I think it's time he and I talked."

I'd been thinking of him since our excursion to Wales last night. Early this morning? Whatever. And even though I didn't have full faith and credit in visions and divinations, it would still be silly of me to ignore Hedwig's warning.

Hazel shook her head, looking crestfallen. "I can't. Finals are in two weeks. I told Quincy we'd study for herbology together. But... if you really need me..."

I shooed her away. "Go. Go study and tell me all about the plants that can kill me. I can find one professor on my own."

Hazel gave me a quick hug. "Watch your back," she whispered.

I didn't know if she was warning me about Killough or Ophelia. The point stood for both of them.

I nodded and we went off in different directions. Killough wasn't in the herbology classroom, which wasn't surprising since it was Saturday. And he wasn't in his office. Also not surprising. I didn't know where his apartment was, which left me stumped.

What did professors do out of work hours?

The only professor I knew well was Bane, and I knew what I wanted him to do outside of work. Or whom, to be more exact. But I somehow couldn't picture Killough getting his freak on with a student when classes ended.

I headed up to my room, taking the stairs two at a time. It took me several minutes to find the tools I needed, but once I did I cleared a space in the center of my room and plopped down on the floor.

I quickly sketched a basic floorplan of the academy on my pad of note paper and unwound the silver chain from my scrying pendant. I didn't have any personal item of the professor's, but he was the only vampire at the academy. If I aimed my scrying spell at the closest vamp, it should send me his way.

I hoped.

I closed my eyes and evened my breathing. I held the pendant over the notepad and chanted my spell under my breath. My eyes flew open when I felt the chain tug on my fingers.

"Yes!" The chain swung in a lazy circle, the vee of the Aries symbol on my pendant pointing to the left edge of the paper. I moved my hand, following the pendant, letting it direct me. The pendant jerked, stabbing into the paper, and I marked the spot.

The pool. Which seemed odd. Consider it my own stereotyping, but I just couldn't picture a vampire swimming. Or sunbathing. But what the hell did I know?

I shoved the pendant and make-shift map in my pocket and hurried out of my room and toward the exit outside. The sun made me squint although its rays didn't hold the same heat they had a month ago. The soft splashing of someone slicing through water grew louder as I approached the pool.

I paused by the metal gate. The pool and surrounding patio were empty except for the lone swimmer. There were flashes of thick biceps, a muscled back, before the vamp disappeared under the water to flip into the next lap.

Something was wrong. Instead of long blond hair, the swimmer had dark locks and looked much too tan for Killough. I pulled out my pendant and map, did the little scrying spell again, and it still showed the pool as vamp headquarters.

The man grabbed the edge of the pool and propelled himself out to standing. Swim trunks clung wetly to toned thighs, and beads of water clung to a beautiful, broad back. The man flicked his hair, droplets of water flying, and turned.

Dante raised his hand, smiling when he saw me. "Hey, Delaney. You coming for a swim?"

I looked from Dante to my map and back to Dante. I scraped my teeth over the inside of my cheek. It didn't make sense. "I swear I did this spell right," I muttered.

He sauntered up, rubbing a towel over his head. "What spell?"

I held up my little map. "I wanted to talk to Killough so I scried for a vampire. But it brought me here, to you."

He stilled, his face draining of color.

"Dante?" I reached for the latch to the gate and pulled it open. "Are you okay?"

"You scried for a vampire?"

"Yes, but I must have screwed up." I chuckled. "Because you…." If possible, he went even whiter. "You're freaking me out. I mean, I know you're not a vamp." He was the most open of my men. The one I was probably closest to. We didn't have secrets. Besides, he'd been between my thighs, inside my body, and he'd been very much warm and alive.

I poked him. "You trying to tell my you're one of the undead," I teased.

He swallowed, his Adam's apple bobbing.

"Dante?" I looked back at my map, my heart stuttering. This was all a mistake. I'd just fucked up like I normally did—

"I'm sorry." His voice was a hoarse rasp. "I never meant to keep it from you."

I stepped back, my hips pressing against the metal gate. "What are you saying? Because I know you can't be saying what it sounds like you're saying. That you're—"

"My father is a vampire," he whispered. "I'm half-blooded. You're scrying spell worked. It found me."

# Chapter Twenty

I rocked back on my heels. He hadn't told me. Dante had slept with me. Fought beside me. Been the one man in my life who'd I'd thought I'd known everything about.

And he'd lied to me.

It was worse than the betrayal of tasting unsweetened chocolate for the first time as a child. I'd seen that block of chocolate in the pantry, snuck a nibble, and the memory of that acrid, horrific taste had lingered in my mouth for days.

The taste in the back of my throat got more bitter. I pressed a hand to my belly, sure I was going to be sick. A vampire. An undead. And he'd never told me.

I turned, fumbled with the latch of the gate, and shoved my way out.

"Delaney, wait—"

I slammed the gate closed between us. "I can't talk to you right now." I was probably overreacting. Probably being an anti-vamp bigot. But all I wanted was honesty. I understood when he hadn't told me about being undercover. He hadn't known me yet. But he did now. We'd been intimate, and he hadn't told me.

My feet ate up the gravel path, started to run. I felt his gaze burning into my back until I turned around a bend. I left the path and ran through the forest, slapping at the branches that got in my way.

I'd fought the undead before. Thanness had created an army of them to attack us. The horror of their slack faces and vacant eyes still haunted my nightmares. And Dante was one of them.

I swiped at my cheeks. Okay, now I knew I was being a bigot. Dante was nothing like Than's grotesque creations. And vampires were accepted, respected members of the magical community.

But I couldn't stop running. Couldn't turn around and let him talk to me. Not yet.

I didn't know where I was going, had no destination in mind, but when I stumbled onto the doorstep of

Gareth's gym, it wasn't a surprise. I knocked. No answer. Tried the door. Locked. I stifled a sob. I needed Gareth to be here. It might sound weak, but I wanted him to hold me for a couple of minutes. Be a source of comfort while I pulled myself together.

I pounded on the door, my palm flat against the wood. "Please," I whispered.

The door swung open.

I didn't question it. It seemed like Gareth's home knew when I needed access. I'd wait for him to return. And maybe by that time, I'd have my shit together and could talk about it rationally.

The gym was silent, still except for the dust motes that danced in the light beams streaming in from the windows. I pulled my battle axe from the wall, letting the weight of it in my hands calm me. I gave it a couple of twirls, feeling myself start to center.

A raised voice had my head snapping to the left. Muffled sounds came from behind the door that led to Gareth's private chambers. Maybe he'd been in the shower and hadn't heard my knock.

"Gareth?" I pushed open the door to his cottage and crept through. My gaze bounced over the walls, the floor, the furnishings. It was a good-sized living room, sleekly designed with lots of leather and black slate. Even the sheepskin rugs on the floor were black. His design style could best be described as utilitarian meets undertaker. It was sexy, brutish, and basic, just like Gareth.

"She can't... there's no point..."

I tiptoed to the next door. I didn't want to interrupt him, but I also didn't want to leave. I needed Gareth.

And then I couldn't leave. My brain wouldn't let my feet move. It wasn't the current of dark power that pushed through me when I stood in the doorway to his bedroom. And it wasn't the sight of Gareth in nothing but his black jeans. He stood in front of his wall, talking to what I assumed was a projection or Pic Portal. I could just see a hairy leg ending in a hooved foot on the person Gareth was talking to. Waves of malevolent energy poured from the room, making my skin go clammy and my breakfast churn in my stomach.

I'd never felt anything like it. It felt like pure evil. And it was chatting with Gareth.

I wanted to run, but my feet had become leaden. My body sluggish.

"Will she need to be neutralized?" The voice was deep like Gareth's but had a sharp edge to it. I didn't think that old saying about sticks and stones applied to whatever the hell was in Gareth's home. Its words could slice a person to ribbons.

"No. Not yet anyway." Gareth crossed his arms, the muscles in his back tensing. Outwardly he appeared as detached as ever. But after months of sparring with him I could tell he was on edge.

"She could be an interesting test case." The clawed foot tapped against a white marble floor, the sound coming through the projection clear as day. Wherever this thing was, it looked fancy. "To see what repercussions her death would bring."

I shifted my grip on the axe handle, my palms grown slick. I didn't like where this conversation was going. What it might say about Gareth. Any moment he was going to tell that thing to fuck off. Tell it to—

"Perhaps." Gareth scratched his cheek. "But Jones would be more than just a normal test case. She wouldn't just be any witch I kill. The people who think she's the Chosen One would take it... badly."

The axe fell to my side, the blade slicing a hole in the leg of my jeans.

What.

The ever-loving.

Fuck.

"You may be right." The monster sniffed. "And this point may be moot. For now, watch and wait. And let me know what you discover."

Gareth bowed deeply. "As you wish, Father."

My heart thundered in my chest. My blood raced through my veins. If they said anything else, I didn't hear it. The part of my brain that was still firing was screaming at me to run. To put as much distance between myself and Gareth as humanly, and witchly, possible.

But my feet didn't move. I stood there like an idiot, watching as Gareth waved his hand and made the projection disappear. Waiting until he turned, until his eyes flared wide as he caught sight of me.

"Delaney," he whispered, his voice hoarse.

I shook my head. I didn't want to hear it. And finally, my feet could move again.

I spun and staggered down the hall to his gym. I knocked the door open with the flat side of the axe blade, twisted it so I could hurl it at the far wall.

Gareth blinked into existence right in front of me. His bare chest pressed against the blade, cutting his flesh, a bead of blood rolling down to his ripped stomach.

"Don't go," he said. "Whatever you think you saw—"

"Saw?" I croaked out. "It was what I heard. I thought you were my friend. More than my friend. I thought...." I ducked my head, my eyes burning. I could be a real idiot sometimes. Why had I trusted these men so easily?

Dante was lying. Gareth was planning on killing me. I didn't even want to find Bane. I didn't think I could take it if I found out he'd betrayed me, too. My heart was cracking into pieces, pieces I didn't think could ever be stitched back together.

"I thought I could trust you." My nails dug into the axe handle. "But you're just another lying bastard. Someone else I have to worry about coming after me. Why did you even pretend to like me?"

His tattoos rocketed across his skin. "How did you know what we said?"

I huffed. "I have ears, don't I?" At that moment, I wished I hadn't. I wished I could be that oblivious girl who still thought the men in her life actually gave a fuck about her.

He brushed the axe aside and stepped into my space. I should have been scared. I'd overheard him talking about killing me. But I just didn't have the energy for fear.

"We weren't speaking English, Delaney. Not anything human. How did you understand us?"

"Uh, I failed Spanish in high school. Shit, I barely passed English." I pressed the heel of my palm against my eye. "I'd think I'd know if I could speak a foreign language all of a sudden."

"What did you hear?" He gripped my shoulders. The pupils of his eyes narrowed into oblong slits.

"You talking about killing me, but how it might piss off the people who think I'm the Cho—"

"You understand Chluxto." He rocked back on his heels. "Can you understand me now?"

I shrugged out of his grip. "Of course I can understand you. What the hell are you talking about?"

"I just switched to my father's tongue." He ran a hand over his shaved head. "I'm still speaking it. Only those with lower world blood are supposed to be able to understand it."

My heart clogged my throat. "Are you saying I'm part demon?" Jesus, if that was true, my mom had even more secrets than I'd thought.

"Perhaps. Or something else. Something special." He reached for my cheek, saw my expression, and let his hand fall away. "I know what you think you heard, but you're not the one I betrayed, pet."

"You have about two minutes to explain." I started to cross my arms over my chest, almost cut my chin off, and put my arms down, gripping the axe with both hands instead. I hated this. Hated that I suddenly felt all kinds of uncomfortable in Gareth's presence.

"I was speaking to Lucifer—"

"Lucifer is your father?" I was gaping like a fish on a hook but I couldn't help it. Gareth was the devil's son, and that marble floor... I'd been looking into the devil's home in hell.

"He's sired over four thousand children. It doesn't make me special."

I didn't feel like arguing that point. Not now. I swirled my hand in a continue motion.

"Lucifer's finances have taken a blow recently. To make up the shortfall, he's supplying mercenaries to someone in order to form a witch army. Your missing students."

"He's kidnapping them?"

Gareth shook his head. "They go willingly. For a large sum of money, I assume. My father is working with someone on the academy's council to find the best prospects. Those witches and warlocks who wouldn't say no to causing a little mayhem if the price was right.

But who he's selling this information to is anyone's guess."

He stepped close and cupped my cheek. This time, I let him.

"He thinks I'm working for him, but I'm trying to find out who is forming an army. Who wants to start the war that destroys the magical realm? He thinks I'm here to keep an eye on the Chosen One and see if you'll interfere in his profit-making endeavors."

"And kill me if I do."

He nodded. "But I'm really here to keep an eye on him."

If anyone knew about crappy fathers, it was me. But still, I didn't know if I could betray my dad outright. What Gareth was doing took guts. And considering his dad was the devil, balls of steel.

"Does your dad not care that he's starting a war?"

"No. Not as long as there is money to be made. Politics have never interested him. It's the man who is forming the army we need to worry about."

"Who is worse than Lucifer? No offense," I added.

"None taken. Lucifer might run hell but he's nothing more than a bureaucrat. Humans have a distorted view of him." He stroked his thumb along my cheekbones. "Do you believe me, pet? Do you believe I would never hurt you?"

I turned my face into his palm, like a cat snuggling into its master's caress. "Yes." I sighed. If one of my men killed me, I'd deserve it for being such a trusting idiot. But God help me, I did believe him.

He stepped closer, his bare feet nudging my boots. He threaded his fingers into my hair and tugged. "And you aren't going to leave me?"

"Would you let me?" I scraped my teeth over my lower lip. He tugged my hair again, and a burn started low in my core.

Gareth lowered his head. His lips ghosted over mine. His pupils darkened his eyes. "Never."

"That's good," I whispered. "Because I—"

He slid his tongue between my lips, shutting up whatever pointless thing I was about to say. He tasted of cinnamon and fire, of brimstone and heaven. I scraped my teeth over his tongue, grinning when he growled. He tasted perfect. He tasted right.

And the last of my concerns flitted away.

# Chapter Twenty-One

*Gareth*

She ran her hands over my shoulders. Every inch of skin she touched was a controlled burn. The blade of the axe nicked my waist, and I pulled it from her hands and tossed it aside without breaking the kiss.

Hades, her kiss. Her mouth was everything a demon had ever been warned about. Sweet. Bewitching. Soft. It made a man want to sink into it, disappear, and never come up for air.

That little fuck Dante had tasted Delaney's kiss. The thought had me gripping her hips, pulling her tight to me. I couldn't lose her. Couldn't lose this.

It was a wire I walked with my father, giving him enough to make him believe I fought for him while keeping Delaney safe. There might come a time when I'd have to take more aggressive steps to ensure her protection, steps she might not forgive me for. But until then I would enjoy her sweetness.

"Gareth," she breathed against my lips. She said my name like it was magic. Like it was a prayer. Normally demons didn't involve themselves with prayers, but the reverence in her voice sent all my blood straight to my cock.

I grabbed her ass, lifted her until she wrapped those long legs of hers around my waist. Until her warm cunny was nestled against my erection.

I bit her shoulder. Not hard enough to break skin, at least not through her shirt, but enough to stop me from losing control and spilling like some untried angel.

She whimpered.

I wasn't making it to my bed. I dropped to my knees, taking us to the mat. She deserved more than this. More than a rut on my gym floor. She deserved everything. She was so pure it almost hurt to look at her.

But what she deserved and what I could give were two very different things. I grabbed the neckline of her shirt and ripped it down the middle, exposing a turquoise bra and quivering stomach.

I let my fingers follow my eyes, trailing them over the rounded mounds spilling over the cups of her bra and down around her navel. "So fucking soft." I was used to bodies that had been hardened in the lower world. Everything was hard down there. Bodies. Minds. Souls. That I got to experience this softness even once was a gift.

Once wouldn't be enough. I wanted it forever.

She grabbed my hand. "I'm not soft. I've trained for years and become a tough fighting machine." She tried to make her point by nipping my finger.

My lips twitched. If she wanted to think she was hardened, it was cute. And for a human, she was. But her body was so easily broken. Her flesh so easily split.

My chest burned. I'd never felt the burden of duty before, but I knew without a doubt it was my duty to protect this woman. I grabbed her wrists and pinned them over her head, settling my body over hers. To protect, and to worship this sweet body, to make her scream in bliss.

"You think you can take me, demon?" Her eyes narrowed playfully, even as she hooked one leg over mine and rubbed against me.

A growl rumbled from my chest. "I know I can."

She posted her other leg. Thrust her hips. And flipped me to my back, her warm body covering mine like a blanket.

She looked so proud of herself I didn't have the heart to tell her I'd only used half of my power to resist her move. Maybe only one-third. One tenth? Still, her move was impressive even if I let her pin me.

"I still have your hands." I pulled them wide, forcing her body to lower until her face was hovering above mine. I scraped my teeth along her jaw, sucked at a patch on her neck.

Her breath stuttered in her lungs.

"What do you think you can do to me without the use of them?" I asked. Her scent was clouding my mind. I throbbed so hard I ached. I needed this woman, this human, like no other.

She bit her bottom lip. "Wouldn't you rather see what I can do to you with my hands?"

My fingers released their grips faster than my father escaped a woman's bed.

She palmed me, rubbing over the fly of my jeans, and it wasn't enough. We tore at each other's clothes. Ripped them from the other's body. She marked me with her nails. I scored her with my teeth. When she lay bare before me, my heart stilled.

She was beautiful. From the stubborn tilt of her chin to the callouses on her knuckles.

And she was mine.

She spread her legs in invitation, and I inhaled deeply. Later, I would explore her bounties more fully. See if she tasted as good as she smelled. But my body wouldn't wait. I sank into her, inch after inch, my brain whiting out in pleasure.

"Oh God." Delaney lifted her hips, taking me deeper as she arched her neck.

I bit her again, making sure that mark would last a while on her flesh. Let everyone know who she belonged to. That pup Dante wasn't a real threat, but I'd seen the way Bane had looked at her.

He couldn't have her.

Pleasure streaked along my cock. Her walls were wet and hot and tight and it took all of my discipline not to rut into her and find my own release. But I was Yithu Gareth Daxti, demon of the Asom realm, son of Lucifer. If there was one thing I knew well, it was how to pleasure a female.

I hooked her knees over my shoulders, fucked her deep and hard. I pounded into her fast, until she was mewling and clawing at my back, then eased out, taking it slow, denying her the release she craved.

She cursed me. Dug her nails into my chest. Slapped me at one point. But she had no leverage. No way to take control. And when she finally rippled around me, squeezing me so hard I worried for my dick, her scream of pleasure was the loudest, sweetest sound I'd ever heard.

I buried my face in the crook of her neck. I pounded home twice more. Ecstasy raced down my spine, gathered in my ballocks, and exploded out of me. I came harder than ever before, painting her sheath with jet after jet of cum.

My muscles felt broken, and I sagged against her body.

She gasped for breath. "Oh God. Oh Jesus. That was..."

"I know." I licked sweat from her breast. It had been all that and more.

She smacked my shoulder. "Don't get cocky. I've had better." She pursed her lips. "Maybe."

I pushed up on my arms and glared down at her. "Liar."

She sniffed. "Besides, you ruined my shirt. I have to walk back to my room half-naked."

That wasn't happening. I lifted her shredded shirt. But yeah, this wouldn't cover anything. "Stay here tonight."

"That just delays the problem." She scooted out from underneath me and gathered her clothes. "I can't stay here forever."

Forever. I cocked my head. That didn't sound—

She punched my shoulder. "Not happening."

I rolled to my feet. That was a fantasy I'd tuck away for another day. Grabbing her arm, I hauled her to her feet. "I'll have something you can wear."

She bit her bottom lip and even though I didn't think it was possible yet, my cock twitched in renewed interest. "One of your soft, stretchy black tees?"

"Yes." They were the only shirts I owned, but she could have the whole damn lot. She already wore my marks. My seed. I glanced from the faint bruises at her throat to my cum sliding down her inner thighs, going full hard.

My shirt covering her body was just the icing on the damn cake.

She was mine. She could have anything she wanted. My possessions. My body. My life.

But I couldn't give her my heart.

She rolled up onto her toes and butterflied a kiss across my jaw, making my chest squeeze in a very un-demonlike way.

After all, she'd already taken it.

# Chapter Twenty-Two

*D*elaney

His shirt hung to my mid-thigh, and even with my boobs, still wasn't tight around my chest like it was on Gareth. I'd known he was built, but until I'd felt all that muscle beneath my hands, all his power surging into me, I hadn't really *known* it.

But the tee smelled of him. Him and laundry detergent. I held the sleeve up to my face and inhaled.

I'd just had sex with Gareth. And it was everything and more than I could have wanted.

"Here. Your pants." Gareth used his teeth to cut the thread that attached the top button to the needle he held. He tossed my jeans to me. "That button should hold for the next ten years. Or until we do that again."

He smirked from the leather sofa in his living room, and I couldn't find it in me to make a snarky reply.

Damn. I pursed my lips. He'd fucked the snark right out of me. I hadn't thought it possible.

"Thanks." I considered my jeans. I could put them on and wobble back to my room for a rest my body desperately needed. Or I could drop the pants, slide on top of Gareth's lap, and go for round two.

The pants fell to the floor. "Gareth, I don't suppose—"

The door that led to the gym flew open. "Delaney! There you are." Dante's face was flushed, his chest heaving, as though he'd just run a marathon. Or been running around the academy grounds looking for me.

"Dante." I snatched my jeans back up, holding the waistband to my hips and trying to hide my bare legs.

"Jesus." Dante raked his hand through his hair. "I've been looking everywhere for you. Even if you won't talk to me about, about, well, you know, I need to tell you about what I found in the council's computer files. I need..." His gaze flitted from me, to Gareth, back to me and my half-dressed state.

I could see the exact moment when it clicked in his brain what he was looking at.

"Did you..." He took a step forward, his shoulders bunching towards his ears. "Did you... sleep with him?"

Gareth rolled to his feet and stepped behind me. "There was no sleeping involved." And as if he hadn't pounded the point home hard enough, he rested his chin on my shoulder and slid his hand up my side until he cupped my boob.

I smacked his hand away. "You're not helping."

A divot puckered his forehead. "Was I supposed to?"

A low, rumbly sound came from Dante as he took a step closer. It chilled my blood. It was the sound of a volcano ready to blow. My body instinctively leaned back, bumping into Gareth.

Where another vicious growl erupted, scaring the piss out of me. I was the meat in a snarly sandwich of two pissed off, possessive men.

No, not men. One demon and one half-vamp.

I sidled my way out from between them. "Look. Let's discuss this like—"

Their two bodies clashed, the force of their impact disturbing the air and lifting a strand of hair from my face.

They moved almost faster than my eye could track. But I heard each snarl and grunt. Each blow that landed.

"Jesus." I shook my head, not knowing if I was more disgusted over their behavior or guilty over mine. All I knew was this had to stop before they killed each other.

"Enough!" I used my loudest, sternest, most bitch-do-what-I-say-now-or-else voice.

It had zero effect.

I marched up to them, ducked under one swinging limb, and shoved Gareth's shoulder. "Stop this, you idiots. You—"

An elbow filled my field of vision. Before I could do anything other than think 'oh shit,' it clocked me in the left eye. I took a wobbly step back then fell onto my butt. I pressed my hands to my face and tried to breathe through the dizziness and pain.

"Delaney." Dante dropped to his knees. "Are you all right? Let me see." He reached for my face.

Gareth shoved him aside. "Of course she's not all right. You hit her." He tugged my hands from my face and tilted my chin up, examining the damage from all angles.

"Me?" Dante rose, his fists clenched. "You're the asshole that hit her. I swear to God if she has any permanent damage, I will rip your arms from their sockets and shove them so far up your a—"

"Enough." This time, my voice must have had enough bite because both men fell silent and turned to look at me. "I will not have two grown men fighting over me." Words I never thought I'd say. A small, childish part of me couldn't help but thrill at the fact, however.

Two incredibly sexy men were beating the ever-loving shit out of each other. Because of me.

I ignored the tingle in my nipples, and I waved my hand at the bruises that were raising on Gareth's torso, at Dante's torn clothes. "You could have killed each other. We're supposed to be friends. Working together. And I know I'm the one who messed that up—"

"No." Gareth rose, stalked from the room but quickly returned with an ice pack and a small towel. He wrapped the towel around the pack and pressed it to my cheek. "This isn't your fault. You've chosen me now, and the pup will have to accept it."

I swallowed, the back of my throat burning. If only it were that simple.

"Is he right?" Dante's face was pale. "Do you want to be with him?"

I didn't answer. It was more complicated than a yes or no.

"Is it because..." Dante looked to the side. "...I'm half vampire?"

Gareth stiffened. "What?"

I pulled my legs in to sit cross-legged, then pushed to stand. Gareth and Dante each leapt forward and grabbed one of my elbows as I teetered.

I pressed the ice to my sore eye and focused on my feet with my other. "This is such a mess." I drew a small triangle on the floor with my bare toe. "This isn't because you're part vamp. I'll admit, I was hurt when I found out. Hurt because you never told me." And I still was. But this was Dante. He was still sweet and amazing even if he was part undead.

I jerked my head up. "The ceiling. You weren't spelled. You were floating upside down because you're a vamp." Oh God. "You were going to turn into a bat."

He blew out his cheeks and huffed. "No. We can't turn into bats. Or any animal."

Hmph. I didn't know if I was relieved or disappointed by that bit of info.

"But we can levitate," Dante said. "And... I haven't quite got control of that. It usually only happens when I sleep." He cleared his throat. "This whole thing is kind of new for me. I only found out two years ago that my dad was a vampire. It had always just been me and my mom. I don't think she wanted to ever tell me, but she knew my transformation would be starting soon. She had no choice."

Gareth grunted. "A vampire and witch mating can produce very powerful warlocks. Maybe you will be useful."

Dante ignored him. "I'm trying to fight it, these feelings I'm having." He stared at my throat, and a shiver danced over my skin. "I don't want to want—" He bit off whatever he was going to say next, but I could guess.

I took a step toward him. "Lots of vampires live normal lives in magical society, though. It's not like in the movies where you go around killing people." That had to be right or else Killough wouldn't be a professor here. "What are you afraid of?"

His eyes darkened. "You found out and ran."

Shame coursed through me. I opened my mouth to apologize, but he wasn't done.

"Vampires might be a part of society, but they're... we're... not fully accepted." Dante closed his eyes and exhaled a long breath. "And I don't ever want to do anything to hurt you."

Bite me. He didn't want to bite me and drink my blood. And I wasn't necessarily thrilled with the idea, either. But I couldn't let him think I was disgusted by him. Couldn't let him think that he was somehow less because of who he was.

I tried to organize my thoughts. Tried to figure out the best way to say all I was thinking. But I couldn't think my way through this, I realized. I had to just say what I was feeling. "You're right. I did run. It scared me. Not only you being part vamp, but that you'd kept it from me. I didn't think we had any secrets."

"Delaney—"

"No." I held up my hand. "Let me get this out. I was hurt and I guess I ran here looking for a little comfort from Gareth. But that doesn't mean that I don't have feelings for you." I looked at Gareth and shrugged. "And you. I like both of you, and I'm scared to death I'm going to ruin everything. I don't want to hurt either of you. But I can't choose. You're both too important to me."

I dropped my gaze back to the floor. Now didn't seem the time to mention that these confusing, swirling, nipple-tingling feelings I was having weren't just limited to the two of them. That Bane featured prominently in them, too. But I'd probably disgusted them enough by admitting to liking two men. No need to up the ick factor.

"You like both of us?" Gareth scratched his smooth head. "Even after what I just did to you?"

I snort-laughed. With Gareth, it was all so basic. We'd had great sex so, of course, I should choose him.

"What does that mean?" Dante asked, planting his hands on his hips.

"That I gave her many orgasms."

"You son of a—"

I stepped between them. "Stop. I don't want another black eye."

"She's right." Gareth pinched my chin, and pulled the ice pack away. His eyes narrowed on the bruise I knew was forming. "I'll kiss it and make it better." His breath skated over my skin. His kiss was feather-soft, and even though I knew it couldn't have any medicinal effects, my eye did feel better.

Those low, growly sounds that seemed so strange coming from Dante filled the room.

Gareth huffed out a laugh.

"Delaney needs someone who can take care of her whole body." Dante stood behind me, resting his hands on my shoulders and digging his thumbs into the tight muscles.

I curled into his massage.

He butterflied his lips along my throat. "I can give you everything you need."

Gareth flicked his tongue over the hollow of my collarbone. "Delaney knows what it feels like to have a real demon between her legs. She won't go back to second-best."

The ice pack fell from my hand. They were both right, and both so very wrong. The slight ache between my thighs was a strong reminder of just how good Gareth was. But my memory was excellent, and Dante had rocked my world, too.

And aside from the sex—Gareth latched his mouth around my nipple, dampening my shirt—which right now was *really* hard to not think about, both men were amazing. Strong. Loyal. Moral.

I leaned back into Dante as he smoothed his hand over my stomach and cupped my heat. The back of my eyes burned even as the rest of my body lit up under their attention. "Don't make me choose," I whispered.

It was such a punk move, but I needed them to decide. It would break my heart whoever I lost, but I couldn't make the choice. I could never choose between my men.

They paused. Dante with his hand buried in my underwear, and Gareth with his teeth scoring my breast. They pulled an inch back, and I almost cried at the loss of their touch.

"Please." I didn't know what I was asking for. For this decision to be over with. For the storm in my heart to end. Or for them to put their damn hands and mouth back on me.

My core clenched.

The latter. Definitely the latter.

"This one time." Gareth's face was hard, but he wasn't looking at me. He glared past my shoulder at Dante.

Dante gave one small jerk of his head. "Agreed. And we'll see who gives her more pleasure."

I blinked, trying to clear the fog from my head. "Wait. What?"

Gareth dropped to his knees before me. "I'm going to make you feel so good, pet. Do you want that?" He hooked his fingers in the hem of my panties and slid them down my legs.

I nodded as I stepped free from my underwear. Yes, please.

Dante smoothed his palms up my sides, taking my shirt up and over my head. "And I'm going to make you scream louder than you ever have before. It will be my name you say, me you're thinking about when you come."

I stood between them naked, Dante at my back and Gareth at my feet, as realization dawned. It was the ultimate dick-wagging contest. The who-could-make-Delaney-come-harder competition.

A part of me thought I should probably be offended. It was childish and silly for these men to think they could tip the scales in their favor by sexing me up.

Every other part of me pile-drived that hypersensitive whiner to the ground.

I didn't have to choose. Not yet. And holy shitballs, *two* men? At the same time? I wasn't even sure of the logistics of that, but was damn eager to find out.

Dante put two fingers under my chin, turning my head. He took my mouth, possessing it, possessing me, as he let his hands roam. He skated them over my rib cage, up to my breasts, plumping them as he squeezed.

"Fuck." Gareth's breath was hot on my tight curls. "I don't want that to be hot, but it is."

Dante rolled my nipples, making me arch, and drawing a long groan from Gareth.

Dante drew away from my mouth, using those devilish lips on my ear and throat, allowing me to catch my breath.

Until Gareth lifted my left leg over his shoulder and buried his face in my pussy.

"Oh God!" All the air in my lungs whooshed out as I grabbed the back of Dante's neck with one hand, needing something, anything, to hold onto.

Gareth's lips. On my pussy. His tongue. Sliding up my slit.

I had never felt anything so good. So decadent. It was better than a brownie hot fudge sundae topped with Luxardo cherries. It felt so good it had to be bad for me.

And I didn't give a shit. At that moment, I didn't care about consequences. There could have been a horde of hell-demons knocking at the door to attack, and I'd have told them to wait their damn turn to try to kill me. Nothing was moving me from this position.

Dante eased one hand over my hip, the tip of one finger sliding through my butt cheeks before he found my dripping core. He pumped that finger inside as Gareth worked my clit.

"Hot. Wet. And so fucking ready for me, aren't you, baby?" Dante sucked at a patch on my throat.

I had no words. Couldn't even nod. All I could do was dig my nails into his neck and pray he got my message.

The rasp of a zipper told me he had. "Watch that tongue down there," Dante warned Gareth. That statement earned a growl from my demon, one that shivered through my clit and went straight to my nipples.

Dante grabbed my hips, tilting them back an inch, and notched his length at my opening.

Holy shit. This was really going to happen. I was really going to get—

I moaned as Dante drove his cock deep, filling me so good and pushing me firmly onto Gareth's mouth. The orgasm came fast and hard, shaking my body from the inside out. The one leg I had planted on the floor gave out, but it didn't matter. My men had me. They wouldn't let me fall.

"That one was mine." Gareth kissed his way up my belly. My leg stretched high, but it didn't matter. I was a very flexible girl.

"Like hell." Dante dropped his forehead to my shoulder. "But fuck if I can argue now. You feel so damn good, baby." He thrust in and out of me, his strokes deep and firm. "Need this, need you so bad."

Gareth bit the underside of one breast. "Every inch of you tastes like ambrosia. I can't get enough." With one last nip, he settled back down between my thighs. His eyes were pure black. His tattoos darted over his skin, their motion so fast it made me dizzy.

I grabbed his head, wishing for the first time that he had hair so I could tug it. Control his movements. Bring him back to where I needed.

But I wasn't in control. Not over them, not even my body. As soon as Gareth pressed the flat of his tongue on my clit, I just about broke. "Too much." It was too much sensation, too soon. I couldn't take it.

Gareth gripped the back of my thigh. "No. It isn't." He drew a figure-eight around my nub, making my body jerk in pleasure-pain.

"You can take it, baby." Dante held himself deep, swiveled his hips, before dragging his cock out and pounding back in. "We want you to give us everything."

My body was soft clay, theirs to mold. I gave myself over to them, trusted them to take care of my pleasure.

And I wasn't disappointed.

The tension built quickly. Every time I thought I'd reached the peak, however, I'd plateau, and a new peak would stretch before me. I whimpered in frustration. "Harder."

Dante's balls slapped against my ass. Gareth alternated using his tongue, teeth, and lips on me until I couldn't think straight.

Something sharp raced down the side of my neck, making me shiver. Dante dropped his forehead to my shoulder, squeezing his eyes shut. "Fuck. I need..."

I combed my fingers through his hair. His teeth. His teeth had been the sharp sensation down my neck. I was fucking a vampire and he wanted to bite.

The thought should have scared me. Or disgusted me. Or at least given me one damn moment of pause.

But it didn't do any of that. It felt like the most natural thing in the world. Of course, Dante wanted to bite me. And the pulse in my throat ached to be bitten.

"It's okay," I whispered. I tried pulling his head to my throat, but he resisted. Huh, even with hair I couldn't control my men. Go figure.

Gareth spread my leg wider, lapped at me like he was dying of thirst.

Movement at the door turned my hooded gaze.

Bane stood in the entry, his mouth a round O of shock. But his eyes were burning. With anger. With possession. With lust.

I felt every one of his emotions as we locked gazes. I had two men pleasuring me, yet suddenly it wasn't enough.

"I can't... resist." Dante sucked at my throat, as though giving me a hickey might be enough to satisfy his craving. His thrusts became jerky, his breathing erratic.

Bane gripped the bulge behind his fly with one hand, his eyes never leaving my face.

"It's okay." I reached for Bane. I didn't know if I spoke to him or to Dante or to all of us.

This, whatever this was, was how it was meant to be. It felt too good, too pure. It was going to be messy and hard and confusing as hell, but the four of us were meant to be together. I wasn't supposed to choose. All of them belonged to me.

My hand glowed as it stretched toward Bane. A soft red-gold color that made me think of happiness and rainbows and light.

The muscles in my body tightened. Gareth flicked my clit. Dante stretched me with his thick cock. And Bane ate me up with his eyes. My lungs squeezed. My toes curled.

And Bane turned and walked out the door.

The glow left my hand with Bane's departure, but nothing could stop the orgasm barreling down on me. Not even his rejection.

With a strangled moan, Dante sank his teeth into the curve of my neck. The pain was sharp but fleeting. And then I was flying. The orgasm rocketed out from my core, shot through my body and met with the ecstasy sliding through my veins from Dante's bite.

There wasn't one inch of my body that didn't shatter in sensation. I felt the orgasm everywhere.

I screamed. My fingernails drew blood, and I didn't know if it was from Gareth or Dante. Didn't care. All I knew were the white-hot waves of rapture wracking my body until my mind went white.

I came to my senses lying on Gareth's lambskin rug, Gareth and Dante pressed tight to my sides.

Dante's worried face hovered over mine. "Thank God. You were out for so long, I didn't know..."

"It was only a couple of minutes." Gareth brushed my hair off my cheek. "Hello, pet. Feeling better now?"

I pursed my lips. I couldn't feel my body. I felt deliciously apart from it, like my consciousness was floating on a cloud. I felt so separated, I started to worry. I did still have a body, right?

I concentrated and wiggled my toes. Yep, still there. My fingers worked, too. A slight ache made itself known at my neck, and I touched the spot where Dante had bit me. My fingers came away dry.

"I... my saliva closed the wound." Dante looked away. "My family told me it would, but I didn't know for sure. You're the first person I've bit."

I cupped his jaw and brought his face back to mine. "Don't be ashamed of what you are."

Gareth rolled to his feet. "Don't get your knickers in a bunch, pup. I think it's safe to say she liked it."

Oh boy, did I. But should I? Dante's bite, could it be dangerous? In the moment, everything had felt so right. So perfect. Like it was meant to be. But that was just the hormones and chemicals flooding my body. Dante's and Gareth's touch could become addicting. And while I cared about all of them, I wasn't the type of woman to attach my wagon to one horse.

I looked to the door. Maybe if I had three horses to—

No. Bane obviously didn't want any part of this, and I would always be the woman who didn't know the first thing about how to love.

I cared for my men. I'd even give my life for them, just like I would for Hazel or Quincy. But I knew my limits. A friends-with-benefits arrangement was the most a girl like me could hope for. Really, really tight friends who'd do anything for each other, but nothing more.

*You're a cold bitch, just like your mother.*

Nausea swirled through me. I scrambled for my clothes, suddenly shy in spite of what I'd just done with these two men. Perhaps because of it. It had felt amazing in the moment, but now came the after part. The awkwardness. The recriminations.

Gareth would expect me to choose him. His ego wouldn't allow for any other option. Dante was still working through his shit, feeling guilty over biting me. From the longing glances he was making at my throat, however, it looked like he wanted to do it all over again.

And I... well I didn't know where the hell to go with any of this. There was only one thing I wanted to deal with, and that was making sure Bane was okay. That the four of us were good to go on as we had before. Partners. Friends. The crew who was going to save the world.

I couldn't find a sock so pulled on my sneakers without them and strode for the door.

"Where are you going, pet?"

"Bane saw us." And I couldn't let my selfishness mess up what the four of us had going. We were a team. And he had looked... hurt. I swallowed, tasting bile. "We need to find him."

# Chapter Twenty-Three

It wasn't hard to find Bane. He was in Gareth's gym, pounding on a bag.

I hurried over to him and pulled his hands away from the rough canvas. "Gareth has wraps right over there." I jerked my head toward the shelf of supplies then examined his raw knuckles. "Why aren't you using them? You could get an infection."

He breathed hard but said nothing. Just stared at me, eyes piercing, his button-down shirt clinging damply to his chest, looking sexy as hell.

"I'll get the iodine," Gareth said.

"I don't need any bloody iodine." Bane jerked his hands from mine and stalked to a low bench. He picked up his jacket and slid his arms into the sleeves. "I came here to tell Delaney news I just heard from the headmistress. If she isn't too busy."

The ice in his voice gave me frostbite. "No. I'm not too busy. And I think we all have news to share." Time to get this whole fucking mess out in the open.

Bane crossed his arms. "Dreadmoon has decided that if one more incident occurs here at the academy because of Delaney, she will be rescinding your admission. And what the hell happened to your eye?"

"What?" Any lingering embarrassment was burned away by my indignation. "That isn't fair."

"Regardless, that is her stance." Bane raised his hand toward my face, dropped it. "And if you aren't here under our protection behind these walls—"

"I'll leave with her." Dante stood next to me. His hair was impossibly ruffled from my hands, his shirt wrinkled.

Bane flicked his gaze dismissively over Dante. "We'd all have to leave. Or hide her away somewhere close."

That didn't sound fun. "Let's figure this out before it comes to that. Dante, you said you'd learned something in the council computers. Go."

"There was something in every student's files that wasn't in the files of missing witches and warlocks." Dante frowned, running his hand up the back of his head. "All their psych evaluations had been deleted. I don't know if that's significant, but it's one hell of a coincidence."

"Wait.' I held up my hands. "Psych evaluations? We have to talk to head-shrinks at some point?"

"No." Bane tilted his head. "The evaluations are made without interviews. Why do you think they'd be deleted?" he asked Dante.

"No. Back up." That didn't make sense. Even I knew it was unethical to diagnose people without having even talked to them. I'd learned that in an episode of some TV show I was sure. "How can we be evaluated without meeting with us? And, more importantly, is there a file on me?"

Bane flitted his hand through the air. "The files are compiled through a combination of observation and divination."

"That's messed up." And creepy. I tugged on Dante's arm. "What did mine say?"

"I didn't look." He squeezed my hand. "But I'm sure it was only good things."

Gareth snorted. Bane rolled his eyes. Which was just rude. My psych evaluation should damn well only say nice things about me. I was delightful. And, I might point out, had adapted very well to the idea of magic and that I might be the destructor of the world.

Unless the oracles thought I was going to go nuts sometime in the near future.

I really hated divination.

"It makes sense." Gareth tapped the blade of a knife against his palm, and I blinked. When had he picked up the knife? I examined his bare chest and his low-slung jeans. And where had he kept it?

"Lucifer has to be picking his candidates somehow. He's going through the files, seeing which students would be susceptible to becoming mercenaries." A tattoo crawled up his neck. "The council must be in on it."

There was a beat of silence. "I seem to be out of the loop," Bane finally said.

"Me too." Dante narrowed his eyes.

I gave them a quick run-down of what Gareth had told me earlier. Leaving out the bit about Lucifer being Gareth's father. That seemed like something he should get to tell them.

"You knew." Dante advanced on the demon. "You knew where the missing students were this whole time

I've been looking for them, and you never said a damn thing."

I must be stupid because I hopped between them once again. "He had his reasons. But going forward, we're all going to be completely honest with each other, right?" I waited for each of them to give me a brisk nod before lowering my arms. "So, what's the plan from here?"

"I have a friend in the council." Bane checked his watch. "I'll contact him. See if he suspects any of his fellow council members could be procuring witches for an army. Maybe even get him to do a little undercover work." He grimaced. "It will cost me a bottle of thirty-year-old scotch."

"I need to check in with my lodge." Dante typed a message into his phone before sliding it back into his pants. "They need to have this new information."

"And I'll go to lower world." Gareth cracked each knuckle on his right hand. "See if I can find out more about who is buying these mercenaries."

They looked to me.

I pressed a knuckle into my lower back. Exhaustion had crept up on me and I wanted nothing more than to sleep for the next decade. Tomorrow I'd meet with Hazel and Quincy, see if we could figure something out.

But for now.... "I'm going to bed. With a large plate of brownies." At Bane's raised eyebrow, I shrugged. "I can't think of anything I can do to help right now, can you?"

"Perhaps not," Bane said.

"What are brownies?" Gareth asked.

I shook my head pityingly. What a sad, deprived life my demon had led. "Only the best chocolate dessert ever."

"Hmm. Brownies won't help anything, either." Gareth drew his eyebrows together.

I huffed. It was like he didn't know me at all.

Dante leaned in and kissed my cheek. "I'll have the cook send up some of his salted caramel brownies. A whole batch, just for you."

I threw my arms around his neck. Finally, someone who got me. "I love you."

I froze, my stomach slowly swirling to the floor. Oh. Crap. "I mean..."

"I know what you mean." He smirked. "I love you, too."

Gareth peeled Dante's hands from my lower back. "I love her more."

"Jesus." Bane shook his head and stalked out of the gym.

"Um, yeah." I rolled onto the balls of my feet, the urge to flee overwhelming. There was three times more love talk going on in here than I was comfortable with. "So, I'm just going to leave, too. So, yeah, bye." I raced over the gym mat and out the door. The outside air had never smelled so sweet. And unemotional. And not weird at all.

I didn't wait to see if either of them followed me. They both had their shit to do and hopefully that didn't include talking about what just happened at Gareth's. Not the threesome, not the love talk, I wasn't ready to deal with any of it.

When I was sure neither of them had followed me I slowed my feet and pressed a hand to my chest. My heart raced from my sprint, and was adding some strange twisting, flopping motion into the mix. It wasn't a pleasant feeing.

I blamed Dante. He could have made a joke of my slip of tongue. Could have ignored it. But *noooo*. He had to repeat it. That he—I gulped—loved me.

Idiot.

He had to know I cared about him. Cared about all of them. But that was the limit of my feelings. Sure, I'd proudly stand next to them in any fight. Hell, I'd give my life for any of them. And yes, just being in their presence made my veins feel like they had champagne fizzing through them. They made me feel safe and happy and altogether—

Shit.

I froze. The graveled path I stood on dug through the thin soles of my sneaks. The pool to my right twinkled a deep blue with the lights shining from beneath the water.

My breath came out in jerky gasps. Shit. Was I… in love?

It shouldn't be possible. I wasn't that kind of girl. And the only love I'd ever been shown wasn't something I'd ever want to see replicated.

I forced my feet to move, turning to cut through the pool patio. But these men weren't my father. And I should never compare anything about them to that bastard.

But still. Love? I—

I blinked. Tried to look down at my immobile feet but my head wouldn't move. Nothing moved. Not my fingers or my toes. Only my eyes could swivel about.

And then the tickling sensation started.

A light chuckle broke the still night air. There was a rustle, movement from a bush to my right, and Ophelia emerged into my field of vision, followed by two of her friends.

"That was easier than I thought it'd be." Ophelia raised her phone and snapped shots of me. "Though I shouldn't be surprised. You are a pathetic excuse for a witch."

I managed a sound between a wheeze and a dying goose.

She tutted. "No need to get nasty. I won fair and square." She waved at her friends. "And I have witnesses. And proof." She took another pic. "I really hope you fail C and D because of this and that I will be the witch responsible for getting you kicked out of the Raven Academy."

She circled closer, like a hyena after a wounded gazelle. "You don't belong here."

She disappeared behind my back. Great. Along with the unbelievably irritating sensation of someone tickling me, I now had the heebie jeebies running down my spine, too. Would she stab me? Give me a wedgie? With her, I really had no idea what the attack could be.

I mean, stabbing did seem a bit extreme. Ophelia was a witch with a B to the umpteenth degree, but I didn't think she was actually homicidal.

I hoped.

Her breath skated over my neck, and in my mind at least, I flinched.

"I know it was you who destroyed my purse." Her voice was a soft whisper in my right ear. "You didn't think I'd make you pay? Go home, Jones. No one wants you here."

She sauntered in front of me. With one last snap with her phone, one pretentious-ass hair toss, she called to her friends. "Okay. Job done. Let's go get some of those chocolate-chip cookies cook was baking up."

They laughed as they passed by me.

My hands ached to inflict some damage. To bloody a nose. Christ, I'd even settle for pulling one of the bitch's hair. But I could do nothing. Yet.

"Don't worry." Ophelia's voice floated back to me. "The spell will wear off. Eventually."

And then I was alone. Alone with a horrible, crawly sensation clawing over my skin and the smell of chocolate chip cookies in my nose.

Could I smell them from here or was I imagining that? Tears burned the backs of my eyes. The need to scratch my skin was overwhelming. And I could really use a cookie right about now. I swallowed. I could almost taste one.

In a tree above me, a bird made a series of short, shrill calls. Other birds took up the cry. The tree across the pool shook, a mass of black wings flapping in the branches.

My frustration waned, a pinch of fear taking its place. I'd been helped by a raven before, but something about this scene seemed ominous. Where did all these birds come from? The trees were filled with them. And their calls... The sounds were worse than the effects of Ophelia's spell. I wanted to cover my ears but could do nothing as the cacophony of screeches hammered into my body.

And like a blanket was dropped over the academy, the world went silent.

And I knew, deep in my gut, that the silence was worse.

I closed my eyes and focused on moving my fingers. I strained, my lungs pumping like I was doing squats with a hundred pounds on my back. A bead of sweat rolled down my temple.

Nothing.

Maybe I needed to fight magic with magic. I slowed my breathing, focusing on my intention. But no energy gathered in my core. My only objective was to get the hell out of there, and that didn't seem to cut it for the magical world.

An icy trickle of dread slid down my spine.

And I knew I wasn't alone.

I opened my eyes.

The triplets stood before me.

One of the brother's tipped his head to the side. "Look at that. She's been gift-wrapped just for us."

"Ahnnn..." I honked.

Another brother smiled, but it didn't reach his ice-blue eyes. "It's almost disappointing how easy this job turned out to be."

And he walked behind me, grabbed my hips, and tossed me into the pool.

# Chapter Twenty-Four

I sank to the bottom of the pool, the heels of my feet hitting the cement floor first before the rest of my body slowing toppled over backwards. Chlorine stung my eyes, but I could see three figures standing at the edge of the pool, gazing down at me.

I held my breath. They were going to come get me. This had to be a sick joke. Right?

Right?!!

Oh, fuck. They weren't coming for me. My lungs began to burn. A slight quiver shook my body. I wanted to laugh. I wanted to cry. Ophelia's spell was beginning to wear off. But it was too late. As an athlete, I could hold my breath longer than the average Jane, but not long enough before I had full movement again.

I was going to die.

Those fucklets were going to kill me.

And the quiver that went through my body this time wasn't from fear.

It was from rage.

My stomach churned, went hot. All the hours I'd spent training to save the magical world. The attacks I'd suffered through. The threats against my friends. It was all going to be for nothing. I was going to die in the swimming pool of the Raven Academy.

None of the oracles had predicted that ending.

My entire torso felt like it was on fire. The burn of my lungs, the heat of my power gathering in my center. If I hadn't been in water, I would have fried to a crisp.

My mind clouded, and I didn't know if it was from lack of oxygen or from anger. Didn't care. My back arched as energy flowed through my veins. My fingers stretched wide. And magic shot out of my palms.

I exploded from the pool, my body flying into the air to hover over the water.

Identical looks of shock crossed the brothers' faces as they looked up at my glowing body.

And when I say I glowed, I meant I was shining so brightly I lit up the entire area. Astronauts could have seen me from space.

My body felt wired, alive, and completely under my control. Everything felt under my control. My body. The birds. The weather. The power of my magic flowed through me just waiting for me to give it direction.

I finally realized the source of my magic. It was Bitch Magic. My rage powered it, but it was my need for revenge, my combativeness, that let me master it.

And I'd never felt more in my element.

"Surprise," I said. Energy streamed from my palms, keeping my aloft. It was like my body was one of those airplanes that can take off vertically, hovering off the ground. Even though I hadn't chanted the words, the levitation spell we'd learned to do on a pencil flowed through my body. But instead of the magic pushing the object up, it was pushing against the surface of the water, holding me in the air.

It came naturally, instinctually, and I couldn't understand why I'd had such a damn hard time with a tiny bit of wood. I angled my hands and glided over their heads, softly dropping down to the ground behind them.

Water dripped from my hair into my eyes, and I tossed my head back. "Now, do you want to tell me what that was about, or do I have to beat it out of you?"

They'd turned to follow my descent. The triplets exchanged glances, and I swore they were speaking to each other with their minds. A cool trick, if it wasn't being used to plot against me. They nodded as one, and their hands began to shimmer liquid silver.

"You're a more worthy adversary than we'd assumed." The dickface to the far left took a step closer.

"This is better," the one in the center agreed, taking his own step forward. "We'll enjoy this more."

"That doesn't answer my question, dimwits." I flexed my hands. My power still flowed through me like an electric current. I'd never been so happy to be a witch. And, I suspected, I might be a hell of a powerful one at that. "Is this because of the prophecy? Do you think I'll bring the destruction of the world? Because I can assure you, I won't. I'm working for the good side here."

The third one chuckled. "Good. What an interesting concept. But you misunderstand us. We don't want to stop the apocalypse. We want to ensure it."

Of course they did. Because why wouldn't three descendants of a famous, wealthy witch family not want to destroy everything they held dear? I shook my head. Spoiled, selfish bastards. "Were you responsible for the tree that almost impaled me and my friends?"

"Yes," the triplet on the left said.

"Of course." The middle one took another step closer.

"And the minge attack? Did you send those bugs after me?"

The brothers glanced at each other. One shrugged.

"It's not just us who wants you dead," the third one said. He was the one that worried me the most. He hadn't moved and something about that seemed deadliest of all. "We were sent by the council. Though we would have come anyway." He smiled widely. The space where his left incisor should have been was a black hole in his mouth.

Uneasiness swirled through me. "The Raven Academy's council?"

He nodded. "Our brother is the head. Our family controls it." He dipped his chin, his eyes glowing an eerie red. "And we don't need you interfering with our plans."

I slid a step back. I was still feeling like a badass witch, but it was three against one. If I could get away to gather my own forces, I'd do it. "Just what are your plans? Why would you want to see the destruction of the magical world?"

"Money." The brother on my left paced in a wide circle around me. "Every member of the council is getting a share in the profits we make off of delivering witches to Lucifer. Nobody wants that gravy train to go dry."

"Hey, I like money as much as the next person." I angled my body, trying to keep them all in sight. "But these witches are being used to stir up trouble in the magical world. To start a war. You'll be caught in it, just like the rest of us. If the magical world goes down, so do you."

The middle triplet shook his head. "The entire magical world won't end. The war will cleanse out the witches we don't want." He smirked. "Only the good will die young."

"Uh no." I took a step back, and my butt hit a hedge. "The prophecy doesn't specify who dies. *And* it says I could be the advance guard of war. Wouldn't you like that?" Maybe the totally ambiguous prophecy would work in my favor for once.

The third brother cocked his head. "No, the prophecy states that you will bring peace through war. Still an unacceptable outcome."

I ran the prophecy through my head again. "Nooo." I chewed the inside of my cheek. "It says I'll be the bringer of peace, and the advance guard of war. And. Both. The translation that says bringer of peace *or* the advance guard of war makes more sense to me, but either way, it doesn't say that I'll bring peace through war."

He sighed and crossed his arms. "The second clause is subordinate to the first and modifies it."

The second brother tilted his head. "But there is a comma, which means the advance-guard-of-war clause is nonessential. Perhaps our interpretation isn't accurate."

"It doesn't matter," fucklet number one said. "Nonessential or not, that clause exists to provide further information about the subject of the first. About her."

I rubbed my forehead. Crap, they had to be smart, too? And why hadn't I listened more in English class? Were they right? It wasn't how Bane interpreted it, but maybe he'd never heard of subordinate, nonessential whatsits, either.

And, again, why did prophecies suck so much?

"Regardless, our objective remains the same." The brother on the left began to glow, the silvery light dancing around his hands rippling out to cover his entire body. "Let's end this." He pulled his shirt over his head and reached for his pants.

"Whoa." I held up my hands, palms out. "You're rapists, too?" I really hadn't thought their being killers could get much worse, but it had.

The middle one toed off his shoes. "She really is stupid. I can't believe it's taken us this long to kill her."

I looked for an escape route. "Yeah, I've heard that before," I muttered.

The third one began to disrobe. "At least this time we'll be doing it our way."

My pulse pounded in my throat. My limbs vibrated with the magic swirling through my body. "I..."

The brother to my left fell to his hands and knees. His body rippled, hair sprouting out from his skin. With a pained howl, fucklit number one had become a wolf.

"Werewolves." It gave me an odd sense of completion. This whole adventure had begun with a wolf. It would be rather fitting if it ended with them, too.

My gaze shot to the brother on my right. The one with the missing tooth. And it clicked into place.

"Not just any werewolves." He cracked his neck as his other sibling shifted. "But members of the Allupine pack, the deadliest of them all. We've managed to keep the fact of our wolf blood from the witch community for over two hundred years." His lip curled back, revealing his lost incisor. "And I don't take being defanged lightly."

He bent low, and transformed into a massive gray wolf, with the creepy mustard eyes I'd hoped to never see again.

A branch dug into my lower back. They had me hedged in, so to speak, and it was never good to be surrounded by the enemy. A thread of panic shot through me, but I stomped it down. Bitches didn't panic. They kicked ass and took names.

Or died trying.

With just the shimmering of an idea for a spell in my mind, I gathered my power and shot it through my arms and out my palms. The streams of red-tipped gold magic struck the wolves in their faces and knocked them onto their backs.

I stared at my hands. Huh. Maybe I'd been thinking too hard to try to get my magic to work. Just feeling my way seemed to work better. I'd always gone with my gut in a physical fight, prioritizing intuition over strategy.

And it was time I played to my strengths.

I advanced on the dogs. The wide spray from my hands turned into narrowed beams. One knocked a triplet into the pool with a satisfying splash. Another brother howled as a patch of fur burnt into his flesh.

The third charged.

I swung both my hands in his direction. My magic glanced off his shoulder as he dove. His paws hit my thighs, and I crashed to the ground. I was half in the hedge; my other half covered by a wolf. My magic had stunned him, though, and he shook his head, giving me my opening.

I grabbed his throat, letting the energy flow through my fingers. His fur crackled, singed. The smell of burning fur turned the air acrid. He snapped at me, long strands of drool hanging from his one upper canine, but my grip was too strong.

Two low growls sounded close by. One of the first things I'd learned fighting was to never let your opponents get your back against a wall. But right now, the hedge was working for me. With my wolf blocking the half of my exposed body, his brothers couldn't get close.

I squeezed harder, breathing deep into my abdomen, expanding my energy base.

And the wolf in my hands went up like a box of kindling under a flamethrower.

I jerked back, away from the flames. The wolf howled, shook his body, and the flames surged. His brothers yapped, lunging forward as if to help, before slinking back from the heat. The barbecued mutt stumbled to the pool, fell to its knees, and toppled into the water with a hiss.

I rolled to my knees, peeking into the pool. It wasn't pretty. The charred blob looked like an overcooked marshmallow. It slowly sank to the bottom.

Two furry heads swung my way, and I gulped. "I really only meant to stun him..."

I don't think they believed me. They advanced, one large paw at a time. The energy in my core fluttered. Blipped. And my stomach swirled to the ground.

My guilt was ruining my bitch-itude. And interfering with my magic.

The wolf on the left attacked. I threw up a shield. He crashed into it, and it bounced back into me, causing me to stagger into the bushes. The other brother raked his claws across my hip.

I clasped my hand to the stinging flesh. "Bitch, you fight like a cat."

He pulled his lips farther back, and I smacked his snout.

He blinked in surprise. I didn't have time to enjoy it. The wolves kept pressing their advantage. I threw every spell I knew at them, but my power had weakened. I added in martial moves, front kicking one wolf in the face, giving the other a swinging backhand.

They crowded into me, taking my hits and keeping on coming. My muscles shook with fatigue. My heart thundered. And I accidentally dropped my defense on my right side.

The wolf with a white patch on its flank jumped. His teeth sank into my shoulder, hitting my collar bone, and I screamed.

His brother took out my legs, bringing me to the ground.

Images of Dante flashed through my head. Gareth. Bane. I thought of the way Hazel made me laugh with her snide wit. The way Quincy only spoke when he had something important to say. I had a good life here. Surrounded by an amazing group of people.

And I was about to lose it all. The loss was gut wrenching.

"No!" I threw my hands out, squeezing my eyes tight. I waited for the first slice of teeth into my flesh.

And kept waiting.

I peeled open an eye. Two smoking wolf corpses lay feet away.

I flipped my hands to look at my palms. The remnants of my magic faded into darkness.

I rested my head against the ground and stared up at the sky. My body cooled, the chilled concrete and damp clothes a delicious nip against my skin.

I was still alive.

For one more day at least.

A raven circled overhead, its wings beating in sync with my heart.

My stomach rumbled, and I bit off a hysterical laugh.

I didn't think I'd be getting those brownies any time soon.

# Chapter Twenty-Five

"Delaney, you need to sit down." Hazel waved a dagger about like a monkey did a stick. "You're making me dizzy."

I stalked across Gareth's gym and rearranged her grip so she didn't stab herself. "I can't help it. None of them have answered me yet."

With all of my men off on missions of their own, I'd gone to Hazel and Quincy for help. After making me take a hot shower, Hazel had snuck a gallon of rocky road ice cream from the cafeteria's freezers. There was a reason she was my best friend. With three stolen spoons, she and Quincy had followed after me when I insisted on waiting for my guys at Gareth's.

I'd texted, left voicemail, and even left a hand written note in Dante's room and Bane's office. I'd used Hazel's phone as mine hadn't survived its swim. Hazel had put it in a bag of rice, but I didn't hold out hope.

I paced the mats again. The ice cream had long since been devoured, and I doubted Gareth had anything tasty in his kitchen. I needed something to do with my hands, and eating seemed a good solution.

My hands shook, and I clenched them into fists.

I'd killed three people. And this wasn't like last time, with Thanness. That had been an accident. This time...

I might not have wanted them dead, but my magic had killed them nonetheless. My uncontrolled power had snuffed out three lives.

I stopped in front of a canvas punching bag. I threw a left jab. A right cross and uppercut. My bite wound ached beneath the large white bandage Hazel had slapped on me. In contrast, the sting on my knuckles felt good, satisfying, and I understood why Bane had bloodied his.

The little bit of pain at least let me feel like I had a smidgeon of control, if only over my own body.

Quincy circled behind the bag and held it for me. His warm, chocolate eyes crinkled at the edges as he gave me a small, reassuring smile.

My shoulders unbunched. I nodded to Quincy then turned my focus back on the bag. But instead of ruining my hands, I practiced my lower body attacks until sweat made my tank top cling to my skin.

"You want extra training?" a rough voice whispered in my ear.

Quincy's eyes flew wide so I knew I hadn't missed Gareth walking up. He'd done that annoying popping thing, appearing right behind me.

I spun, my chest heaving. "You're back. Finally. Have you heard from Dante or Bane?"

His forehead wrinkled. "No. Why?"

"The triplets tried to kill me. They said—"

"What?" Gareth's pupils stretched. He flicked his gaze over my body, landing and staying on my bandaged shoulder. "Where are they?"

"By the pool. But—"

Gareth turned on his heel and strode for the door.

I ran after him and grabbed his arm. "They're dead." Bile rose up my throat. I was a killer.

I shook my head. I couldn't think about that now. "It's actually..." I cleared my throat. "Someone should clean up the bodies before a student goes there to swim tomorrow. Or today. Whatever." I ran my hands over my face and cupped the back of my neck. I didn't know how long we'd been waiting in Gareth's gym. It could have been one hour or ten.

I glanced at the window. Still dark. Okay, so not ten. "This is such a mess."

"Tell me what happened," Gareth demanded.

"I was walking back to the school after we'd all... talked." Heat rose to my cheeks and I darted looks at Hazel and Quincy. What the hell would they think of me and what I'd done with Dante and Gareth.

Well, Hazel would probably high-five me and Quincy would be more embarrassed than I was. I cleared my throat. "Ophelia stunned me by the pool."

"Miss Ravencroft is in on this, too?" Gareth clenched his hands into fists.

"Yes," Hazel said.

"No." I shook my head. "She did it for the C and D test."

Hazel tossed her dagger down onto a bench, making both Gareth and I wince. "She's been buddy/buddy with those brothers. And she just happens to stun you immobile right before they come by to kill you?" She snorted. "I don't buy it."

"Valid points." Gareth nodded and turned for the door again.

Jesus, he was going to kill Ophelia. I darted in front of him. "We have no proof of that, and I just don't think she'd go that far. She's horrible, no doubt, but she's more mean-girl than psycho killer. And we have bigger problems to worry about."

"What problems?" Dante stood in the open doorway, a cool breeze coming inside with him. His eyes widened as he took in my shoulder. Blood had started to seep through the bandage. "What happened?" he asked as he rushed forward.

I rubbed my bare arms. I gave them both an abbreviated rundown of my night. "We need to find Bane. He hasn't responded to any of my messages. Maybe he'll answer you guys."

There was a good chance Bane had seen my name on his phone and ignored the texts. My stomach clenched. He'd been angry and disgusted by what he'd seen me doing with Gareth and Dante.

I should have pretended to be Hazel instead of saying I was using her phone. Instead of taking any message from me seriously, he might have thought I was calling him to clear the air.

But that didn't explain why he couldn't take two seconds to read past the 'It's Delaney. My phone broke but I need to talk to you..." to get to the heart of my message. I ground my teeth. And what right did he have to hold my actions against me when he was the one who insisted that there could be nothing between him and me but a professor/student relationship.

That man could really piss me off. He was completely infuriating, bull-headed, and arrogant, and ghosting me was just the tip of the annoying iceberg.

And I prayed that his radio-silence was because he was being his usual stuck-up self. Because if that wasn't the reason...

Dante's eyebrows drew together. "You broke through Ophelia's spell to propel yourself out of the pool and levitate over the water?"

"Yes. Now text Bane."

Dante slid his phone from his pocket. "That's high-level magic, Delaney." He blew out a breath as he typed a message. "We really need to explore the source of your power more."

I already knew. It was rage. Bitchiness. Hate. Which could be a real problem since I was usually a very live-and-let-live kind of person.

And none of that mattered with Bane still out there and unaccounted for.

I turned to Gareth. "Try calling him."

He eyed me steadily as he slid his own phone out. "He's a good warlock. He's fine."

I gave him the 'let's go' motion with my hand. "Did you people not hear what the fucklets said? That the *whole* council was corrupt? And Bane was going to go talk to his *friend*"—I made bunny ears around the word—"about it." Until I heard from Bane, my mind would be circling around the worst possible scenarios. And none of them were acceptable.

The call rang and rang on Gareth's end. Bane's recorded voice repeated the message I'd learned by heart. *I'm not available to talk. Leave me a message and I'll return your call with all due haste.*

Gareth lowered his phone as Dante examined my shoulder. I slapped his hand away when he peeled back the bandage, and he slapped mine right back.

"Let me," he said, an edge to his voice that usually wasn't there.

A horrible thought struck me, one I couldn't believe hadn't come to me before. "I was bitten by a werewolf. Does that mean I'm going to turn into one?"

Dante and Gareth shared a look. One I couldn't decipher and didn't like. "Uh, you shouldn't," Dante said.

"Nine times out of ten there's no infection," Gareth added.

I swallowed. Which left a one in ten chance. I didn't like my odds.

I rolled my shoulders. I didn't have time to worry about that now. Not when Bane wasn't answering his damn phone. "You guys, we need to find him." The back of my throat felt raw. I was probably coming down with something after my unintended swim.

Or maybe it was the start of my transformation into a werewolf. Maybe it started with flu-like symptoms.

Or my throat ached because I was about to start bawling because Bane wasn't answering his *damn* phone. I sucked in choppy breaths. He had to be all right. His friend hadn't betrayed him. It was going to be fine. Gareth was right. Bane was a strong warlock. And not someone to be easily taken by surprise.

"I'll try summoning him magically." Gareth closed his eyes, exhaling a long, slow breath. A tattoo peeked out from behind the collar of his tee shirt before disappearing back behind the black cloth.

I glared into each corner of the gym, pissed when Bane didn't appear. He was being summoned, damn it. He should appear.

Gareth sighed and opened his eyes. "Nothing."

"Okay, so he's not answering you, either." I tapped my fingers against my thigh. We'd just have to wait. Bane would be back by morning. It made no sense to worry before then.

"No." Gareth looked at me with a hint of pity. "When you summon a person, you reach out and find their consciousness. A bit like knocking on a door. The person can choose not to answer. But I'm not even finding his door. His consciousness isn't here."

"What are you saying?" Dante squeezed my arm, but I shrugged him off. Sympathy was for people who'd suffered a loss. I hadn't lost anything. Not yet.

"I can't sense him anywhere in the world." Gareth dipped his head. "I'm sorry. He's gone."

Quincy sucked in a sharp breath.

Hazel came to stand next to me. "I'm sorry, Delaney."

"No." I shook my head. "There's nothing to be sorry for. He's not dead." I looked at my friends, at their disbelieving faces. "He's not. Unless and until we find his body, he's alive. Got it?"

They all murmured in agreement, but it didn't sound all that believable, even to my desperate ears.

"So what do we do?" Quincy asked.

I planted my hands on my hips. "Gareth, you said Bane isn't in this world. But maybe he's in another one. Can you check the lower world for him?"

He nodded. "And I have contacts in upper world. If he's there, we'll find him."

"My lodge can send out seekers." Dante took my shoulders. "We'll find out what happened to him."

I locked my gaze on his. "We'll find him," I corrected. We weren't going into this with a defeatist mindset. That was the easiest way to lose a fight.

And this was going to be a fight. Because finding Bane was only step one.

"Hazel, can you and Quincy do research on the council members?" I took Dante's hand off my shoulder but held onto it, letting its warmth infuse into my skin. "I want full backgrounds. Who they are, where they live, when they eat breakfast, everything and anything you can get."

"Detective work." She jerked her head at Quincy. "We can do that. You'll have full dossiers by the end of the day."

I almost smiled. And I had no doubt they would. When Hazel put her mind to something, she got shit done.

"What are you thinking?" Dante asked me.

"I'm thinking that finding Bane is only the first step. After that, we'll have the council coming for us. We need to cut them off at the head."

I took a deep breath and looked at all of them. Everyone I cared about was in this room except Bane. But we'd get him back. And then...

"The Raven Academy is under threat," I said. "The council that is supposed to help our students is preying on them. I want to save our school."

I firmed my shoulders, decision made. "We're going to launch a coup."

And God help anyone who got in our way.

# Sneak Peak of Magic Misrule

“Does he have it?”

Gareth gave a long-suffering sigh. “If he had it, he would end his travels.”

I peeled open one gummy eye. Dante’s body still floated inches above Gareth’s and my joined hands. His eyes were closed, his face serene. Like he’d astral-traveled to a farkin’ island getaway instead of Arzrigoth where he was supposed to be.

My shoulders sagged and I closed my eye again, trying to concentrate on the spell. An island beach sounded awesome right about now. When we got Bane back, and after we'd saved the world, of course, maybe I could convince my guys to take me on a vacay.

Gareth squeezed my hand. The magic flowing between us thickened, his strength shoring up my wavering reserves.

I was exhausted. It had been eight days since Bane had disappeared.

Been taken.

Eight days of Gareth searching the different worlds and dimensions. Of Dante using every contact from his white lodge, trying to trace Bane's whereabouts. Of me, Hazel, and Quincy searching every damn book in the library for a reference to any spell that could possibly make someone's consciousness disappear but didn't mean he was dead.

Because I refused to believe that Bane was dead. I'd feel it if he was. I'd know.

And maybe I was just fooling myself. Because it had been eight days and we'd found nothing. He'd vanished without a trace. Like he'd been...

I swallowed, the back of my throat burning. If the members of Raven's council hadn't gone into hiding, I would have taken great pleasure in beating every single one of them into a bloody pulp until the one who'd betrayed Bane confessed to what he'd done.

"Focus," Gareth murmured.

I tried. We were working a spell that channeled our energy to Dante, allowing him to travel farther than most astral projections allowed. But I couldn't remember the last time I'd slept, my left butt cheek was going numb from sitting cross-legged on my bedroom floor for so long, and I was missing Bane so much my heart actually ached. Concentration was a bit hard to come by.

Gareth rubbed his thumb over mine, sending a comforting tingle along my skin. He'd said the more we touched, the better. Magic was like a network, and the greater the number of connections you had, the stronger it was.

I straightened my spine, sending all my intention into Dante to find Bane. This was a long shot, but it was our last shot. Gareth had convinced a Nahwalli demon, (and I didn't want to know how he did his convincing), to tell him about a rumored underground prison. One that was built to hold the magical. One that hadn't been authorized by any known government.

It sounded like the perfect place a rogue council of witches would send someone they wanted to disappear. Bane had to be there. Now we only needed to figure out where the damn prison was located.

The air shimmered, and my eyes flew open to see Dante's body vibrating. I moved to pull my hand from Gareth's, but he only tightened his grip.

"Don't disturb him now," he said. "Not when he seems to be getting somewhere."

Dante's lip curled in a grimace.

"But..." Astral projection shouldn't hurt. At least, I didn't think so. I'd never done it. But ever since Bane had been taken, my heart had clogged my throat whenever Gareth or Dante were in even the tiniest hint of danger. I couldn't bear to lose someone else I lo— cared about.

Dante panted, the sound loud, animalistic. His incisors stretched, growing long and pointy, and a shiver danced down my spine. I still wasn't used to the fact that one of my lovers was a vampire, and that his bite had been one of the most amazing experiences of my life. But I was getting there.

He snarled, snapped at the air.

"Gareth..."

"Wait."

Dante's nails extended, and my pulse rabbited. "We need to stop this."

"Just wait."

I bounced my knees, nervous energy rushing through my body. This really couldn't be good.

Dante's body spun, like a pig on a spit. When he faced me, his eyes flew open. They were slits, inhuman. He reached for me, those creepy, long nails stretching for my face, and I couldn't restrain a little shriek.

"No." The word was a low growl, barely audible over the thudding of my heart. But it was enough.

Dante blinked at Gareth's command, his gaze clearing. "What...?" He crashed face first to the floor, pinning Gareth's and my hands beneath him.

I tugged my hands free and flexed my fingers. "Are you okay? Did you find him? Where is he?"

Gareth rolled to his feet and stepped over Dante's body. "Give the pup a moment to collect himself. Astral travel is challenging for those less powerful."

Dante rolled to his back and glared up at the demon. "There is no world where I'm less powerful than you."

Gareth smirked. "Whatever you need to tell yourself."

I clapped my hands. "Focus. Where's Bane?" I stared at Dante, willing him to give me an answer I wanted to hear. I wouldn't accept that he hadn't found the prison, that our magic hadn't worked.

Dante gave me a sympathetic look, but that could mean anything. That I was having a bad hair day. That he felt sorry for me that I couldn't choose between my guys. Just because he wasn't answering didn't mean… Oh God. Had he not found the prison? Or had he found it and Bane wasn't in it? Or wasn't alive in it?

My mind raced so hard it went light. I planted a palm on the ground to hold myself steady. "Dante…"

He gripped my shoulder. "I found it. But it won't be easy getting inside."

If it weren't for his hand holding me upright I would have collapsed to the floor with relief. "That's not a problem." Nothing was a problem, not with Bane alive. "I like it hard." Because that meant they had a chance to get Bane back.

Gareth cleared his throat.

Dante smothered his smile.

I ran my words through my head again. My cheeks heated. "Jeez, grow up guys. That wasn't what I meant." Though, yeah, I liked it hard that way, too.

I stood, turning my focus on what needed to be done. "So, we have a location."

Dante nodded.

"And we know the security measures the prison uses."

Gareth shrugged. "We know some of them. My contact could have missed something."

"It doesn't matter. If something comes up, we'll deal with it." I swung my arms back and forth, getting blood flowing through them. I bobbed on my feet hoping if my body felt energized, my mind would, too.

Gareth tilted his head, his gaze dropping to my bouncing boobs. "What are you doing?"

"Getting ready."

"You want to launch a prison break now?" A curving line of blank ink slithered up Gareth's forearm and disappeared under the sleeve of his tee. I was getting better at interpreting the movements of his tattoos, and I think that one meant he wasn't a fan of my idea.

Too bad.

"Yes. Now." We'd need to stop by Gareth's gym and load up on weapons. After that, there was no reason to stall. "I'm not waiting one more minute than necessary to bring Bane back home."

Dante ran his hand up the back of his head, ruffling his hair. "Perhaps we should get a good night's rest and plan our attack tomorrow."

I swiveled my head to face him. "We know our plan. You create a portal to as close to Bane as possible, we grab him, we leave. Now that we know where this prison is, we can put our plan into effect."

"But—"

"No buts." I shook my head. "We're not going to learn anything more about the security systems. There will be no perfect moment. We go now."

Gareth dipped his head in agreement.

Dante clambered to his feet, blowing out a breath. "I don't like it, but I know you won't agree to anything else. Let's do it."

"Want any help?"

I peered around Gareth's ripped body, a grin stretching my lips when I saw Hazel and Quincy standing in my doorway.

Hazel sauntered into the room, Quincy quietly closing the door after them. "So the spell worked?" she asked. "We know where Professor Bane is?"

I nodded. "We're bringing him home."

"Is it wise involving them?" Gareth's tone wasn't unkind, but it was measuring when he looked at my friends. And obviously he found something lacking.

I grabbed a dark hoodie and shrugged it on. "They have better control of their magic than I do, and we can use all the help we can get." I didn't like risking my friends' lives, but we were past the point of such concerns. A war was coming, and without Bane, I didn't like our chances of winning. How many friends were going to die in the battle?

No, the stakes were too high to let my protective instincts get in the way. I strode for the door. "Let's go. If anyone wants extra weapons beside their magic, we'll load up at Gareth's. I call dibs on the battle axe."

I didn't wait to see who followed.

I had a man to rescue.

Read the exciting and sexy conclusion to The Raven Academy now! Get Magic Misrule today!

# About A. Caprice

A. Caprice is the pen name I use when I want to write something a little different. If it's magical, or furry, or has fangs, this is the name I'll write it under. There might even be aliens! I live in Colorado, home of many Big Foot sightings. I used to practice law, but decided I'd rather write about happy endings and forget the mess people can make of their lives. I also write humorous, small-town, contemporary romance novels under the name Allyson Charles and steamy historicals as Alyson Chase.

Printed in Great Britain
by Amazon